Stacey and the Mystery Money

THE BABY-SITTERS CLUB

Stacey and the Mystery Money
Ann M. Martin

AN
APPLE
PAPERBACK

SCHOLASTIC INC.
New York Toronto London Auckland Sydney

The author gratefully acknowledges
Ellen Miles
for her help in
preparing this manuscript.

Cover art by Hodges Soileau

No part of this publication may be reproduced in whole or in part, or stored in a retrieval system, or transmitted in any form or by any means, electronic, mechanical, photocopying, recording, or otherwise, without written permission of the publisher. For information regarding permission, write to Scholastic Inc., 730 Broadway, New York, NY 10003.

ISBN 0-590-45696-2

12 11 10 9 8 7 6 5 4 3 2 1   3 4 5 6 7 8/9

Printed in the U.S.A.   28

First Scholastic printing, August 1993

CHAPTER 1

I never would have believed it. Not in a million years! I never thought that I, Anastasia Elizabeth McGill (otherwise known as Stacey) would have a secret I would have to keep from my closest friends. A secret I could never tell. A secret I would take with me to the grave.

Secrets are fun sometimes. For instance, if you're planning a surprise party for someone. Or when your best friend tells you about a boy she has a crush on. But my secret isn't like that. It's a secret I have to keep because if I don't, I might get someone into trouble. Trouble of the worst kind.

Am I sounding mysterious? Well, that makes sense. This secret has to do with a mystery that my friends and I became involved with, and eventually solved.

It all started — well, let me see. When *did* it all start? I guess I'd have to say it was a few weeks ago, when I was hanging out at my best friend's house after school one day. Claudia and I were in her room, looking over a pile of fashion magazines. We were passing time until our club meeting started that afternoon. We belong to this great club called the Baby-sitters Club, or BSC, which is made up of people who love to baby-sit — but I'll tell you about that later. First, more about Claudia.

My best friend is Claudia Kishi. I've never had a friend quite like her. She and I agree on almost everything, and we are so much alike that it's sometimes hard to believe. We're both thirteen and in the eighth grade at Stoneybrook Middle School. We both love to shop. We both love wild, sophisticated clothes, interesting accessories, and cool makeup. We both love to try out the latest hairstyles. And we're both a little boy-crazy.

"Stacey, can you believe this guy?" Claud held up a magazine, open to an ad for a new men's cologne. A guy was lying on some rocks near an ocean, his face turned toward the sun. He was wearing bleached blue jeans and a white shirt.

"He's a hunk," I said, "but I think he's more your type. You can have him."

Claudia giggled. "Thanks," she said. "I appreciate that." She leaned over the magazine again and flipped some more pages.

I should say that, while Claudia and I are an awful lot alike, we're not *exactly* alike. I think that's what makes our friendship work: we enjoy our similarities *and* our differences. Here's how we're different: I have blonde hair that's usually pretty curly (I perm it) and blue eyes, while Claud has straight black hair and dark, almond-shaped eyes (she's Japanese-American). I'm an only child, and Claudia has an older sister. My parents are divorced, and hers are still together. Claudia has lived all her life in Stoneybrook, Connecticut, the small town where we both live now. But I grew up in New York City, and in some ways I still think of myself as a city girl.

In fact, I visit New York as often as I can, because that's where my father lives. When my parents got divorced, my mom moved back to Stoneybrook (we had lived here for a little while before the divorce) and I had to choose which parent to live with. I hope you never have to make that choice, because it's a really hard one. I'm glad, most of the time, that I live in Stoneybrook with my mother. We get along amazingly well. But it's nice to be able to go to the city to visit my dad — and to stop in at Bloomingdale's, of course.

Anyway, back to the differences between

Claudia and me. There's one other thing: Claudia *hates* school. She's really smart, but she just doesn't like books and tests and reports. The only subject she does well in is art, because she loves it. She's a terrific artist. As for me, I have no problem with school. I do pretty well at everything, but my best subject is math.

Claudia rolled over on her back (she was lying on her bed) and shook a bag of M&M's over her mouth. "Mmmmm . . ." she said. "There's nothing like chocolate!" Then she sat up. "Oops!" she said. "I'm sorry."

"It's okay," I replied, waving my hand. "No problem." I reached for a pretzel and bit into it, wishing just a little that it was a handful of red, green, and yellow M&M's. I used to love M&M's. I used to love all kinds of candy. But that was before I was diagnosed with diabetes. Now I can't eat candy, and sometimes I really miss it. Claudia knows that, which is why she apologized.

I'm basically used to avoiding candy. I'd better be, since I'll have to be careful about what I eat for the rest of my life. See, having diabetes means that my body can't process sugar the way it should. Eating desserts or sweets can make me very, very sick. But just avoiding sweets isn't enough with diabetes. I also have to check my blood sugar frequently, to make sure it isn't too high or too low. And I have to give myself daily shots of insulin, which is something my body should be producing by itself.

Sounds awful, right? Well, it was, at first. But now I guess I've gotten used to the routine, and it doesn't bother me much. I think the part about the shots sounds the worst to most people, but they're no big deal. The part that bothers me most is having to be so strict about what I eat. Once in a while I'd just like to be able to forget about keeping track of every single thing I put in my mouth.

Still, I'd never go back to eating tons of junk food. I'll leave that to Claudia. She loves the stuff. Maybe someday scientists will discover her, and she'll become the first proof that a human being can actually survive on a diet of Ring-Dings, Chee·tos, and Three Musketeers bars.

"Mrs. Kishi," the scientists will say as they interview Claudia's mother. "How did she do it?"

"I can't imagine," Mrs. Kishi will say. "I tried to tell her that junk food was terrible for her, and I tried to keep her from eating it. But she ate it anyway, and I guess she proved me wrong."

Of course, in reality, Mrs. Kishi has no idea that Claud eats so much junk food. Officially,

Claudia is not supposed to be eating any at all. That's why she hides her Ruffles under the bed, her Twinkies behind a curtain, and her Mars bars in her sock drawer. Also officially, Claud is not supposed to read Nancy Drew books, which are her absolute favorites. Her parents would rather see her reading something "more challenging." But Claud loves her mysteries, so they're stashed all over her room, too.

Did I mention that Claudia's room is not very neat? That may be the understatement of the year. Claudia is a slob. But she says she knows where everything is, and that she's happier and more creative in a messy room. Three different art projects are usually going on at any one time, so you might see papier-mâché in one corner, cut-up magazines for collages in another, and beads strewn all over her desk.

Still, I feel comfortable in Claudia's room. Maybe that's because I spend so much time there. Not only because I'm her best friend, but because that's where the BSC meets. Anyway, Claudia's room feels like home.

I picked up another magazine. "Where did you get all of these magazines, anyway?" I asked. "They're great."

"Mom gave them to me," said Claud. "The library was cleaning out their collection. They don't have room for more than two or three years' worth of past issues." Claudia's mother works at the Stoneybrook Library.

I checked the date on my magazine. Sure enough, it was three years old. I hadn't noticed that. It didn't seem to matter, though, since I still had fun looking at the clothes and hairstyles. I turned to a fashion article with photos of two girls and a guy on a picnic. "Claud, look," I said. "Doesn't this guy look a little like Mr. Ellenburg?"

Claudia glanced at the picture. "Woo, woo," she said. "Even cuter."

Mr. Ellenburg was this student teacher who substitute-taught my math class for awhile. I had a pretty big crush on him. He was *gorgeous*, with wavy light brown hair and dimples. I looked at the picture and sighed.

"Do you still think about him?" asked Claudia.

"Oh, once in a while," I admitted. "He was just so mature, you know? That was the best thing about him."

"You mean you prefer mature guys to guys who bring rubber tarantulas to formal dances?" asked Claud with a grin.

She was referring to Sam Thomas, this boy I've been sort of involved with for awhile. He's the older brother of Kristy Thomas, who's the president of the BSC. He's cute, and he's fun,

7

but sometimes he can be really obnoxious. Like the time Claudia was talking about. There we were at the January Jamboree. The gym was beautifully decorated. My friends and I were decked out in super-elegant clothes. (I was wearing this slinky silk gown that belongs to my mother.) Sam (my date) was in a tux, and he looked very handsome, but he was acting like a ten-year-old with that silly rubber tarantula! I actually had to beg him to get rid of it.

"Sam's great," I said. "I usually end up having a lot of fun with him. But — I don't know. I think he and I may be — "

"What?" asked Claudia eagerly. She loves to hear the details of my relationship with Sam.

"Well, it's just that, you know, he has his interests and friends at the high school, and I have mine at our school." Being thirteen and dating a high-school guy who is fifteen isn't easy.

"So are you going to break up?" Claud asked breathlessly.

"Break up?" I asked, surprised. "Well, no. I mean, not yet. I mean, maybe. Oh, I don't know what I mean. I guess we're just going to have kind of an understanding," I said. "Like, we'll still see each other, but we can date other people once in awhile, too."

"Really?" asked Claud. "You've talked about that?"

I nodded. "It's no big deal," I said. "We're taking this very casually."

"You don't seem too upset about it," Claud agreed.

I blushed. "Well, the thing is, I'm not. Because — " I hesitated.

"Because *why*?" Claud said, looking as if she were about to die of curiosity.

"Well, because there's this new guy in my language arts class," I replied quickly, stumbling over the words a bit.

Claudia threw her bag of M&M's into the air. "Yes!" she said. "A new boy!" She grinned at me. "This is exciting. Tell me everything. What's his name? What does he look like? What does he *act* like? Is he in any of your other classes? Why didn't I see him first?"

I laughed. "Terry Hoyt; incredibly cute; nice but shy; yes; you were unlucky," I said. "Those are the answers to your questions, in order."

Claud laughed, too. "So which of your other classes is he in?" she asked.

"Just social studies. He sat right behind me today."

"Did you talk to him?"

"Not really."

"What do you mean, 'not really'?"

"Well, he did ask me if I had an extra pen," I said. "He has beautiful eyes. They're hazel, I guess. Kind of brown and green and gold all mixed together. And he has this shiny brown hair that flops over onto his forehead in the cutest way."

"Hmmm," said Claudia. "Sounds like you have a crush on somebody." Her eyes were bright.

"I don't know if I'd go that far," I replied. "But he is cute. What I can't figure out is how to get to know him better. He seems awfully shy. He blushed when he asked me about the pen."

"Well, we'll figure something out," said Claudia. "First we have to find out more about him, like where he lives and what he likes to do. We can start tomorrow."

Just then, we heard a knock. We glanced up.

Claud's sister Janine was standing in the doorway. "Hello," she said. "I just wondered if I could borrow some Magic Markers for a diagram I'm making."

"Sure," said Claud. "What colors do you need?"

"Well, let's see," said Janine. "I suppose the

carboxyl groups of the amino acids could be green, and the nitrogen could be yellow. Then, when they bind and create linkage in a peptide bond, that would be blue. I'm not sure how to depict the release of the water molecule, but — "

Claudia and I were staring at Janine in wonder. Janine always talks like that. She's an actual genius. She's a junior in high school, but she takes college classes. It's been hard for Claudia to have a sister who's so good in school, but the two of them usually get along very well. Considering how different they are.

"Janine," said Claudia, holding up her hand to stop the flow of technical terms, "I haven't understood a word you've said since 'well, let's see,' but you can have all the Magic Markers you want. Here, take the whole set." She rummaged in a drawer and pulled out a box. "And good luck with your diagram."

"Thank you," said Janine. "And I'd be glad to explain the process more fully, so that you *will* understand it, any time."

"That would be great," said Claudia, as Janine left. "We'll do that sometime." Then she whispered to me, "When pigs fly!"

We cracked up. Then we continued paging through our magazines. For the millionth time, I thanked my lucky stars that Claudia is

11

my best friend. There's just nobody in the world who's more fun to be with. And at that moment, in her room, I never would have imagined that I could have a secret that I would have to keep from her. But it wasn't long before I did.

CHAPTER 2

"Green," mused Claudia. "Emerald green, just like Scarlett's in *Gone With the Wind*."

"I think I'd choose hazel, like Terry's," I said. "He has the prettiest eyes I've ever seen." Claudia and I had moved on to discussing what color eyes we'd most like to have. (Not that either her parents or mine are about to let us get colored contacts.)

"What about violet, like Elizabeth Taylor's?" asked Claud. She had opened her magazine to an extremely fragrant perfume ad. I had just leaned over to look when I heard the front door slam downstairs, and then the sound of feet pounding up the stairs.

"Oh, my lord!" said Claudia. "Is it five-thirty already?" She sat up to look at her digital clock.

I sat up, too, and saw that it was five-twenty-five. "Must be Kristy," I said.

Sure enough, about two seconds later Kristy

Thomas burst into the room. And right behind her were the other members of the BSC. Our Monday meeting was about to start.

Maybe I should take a minute here to explain how the BSC works. It's very simple, really. The idea is to make it easy for parents to line up sitters. Seven of us are in the club, and we meet in Claudia's room every Monday, Wednesday, and Friday from five-thirty to six. Parents can call during that time and set up jobs. We always have plenty of business, since parents like the convenience. (Also, without sounding conceited, I have to add that we are excellent sitters. So it's not *just* the convenience.)

When we started out, we advertised with fliers and with an occasional ad in the newspaper, but now news of our business is spread by word of mouth. Parents who use the BSC and like it tell other parents, and so on.

Kristy is the president of the club for two main reasons. One is that the club was her idea in the first place. The other is that she is a born leader. She knows how to get things done. Also, she keeps on having great ideas that make the club even better. I guess that makes three reasons.

Kristy is short, with brown hair and eyes. Like me, and like most of the members of the BSC, she's thirteen and in the eighth grade.

She's a real live wire, as my mother would say. She's smart and quick and athletic (she even coaches her own softball team for kids) and she can be a little bossy at times. Unlike Claudia and me, Kristy cares nothing about clothes or hair or makeup. She wears pretty much the same thing every day: jeans, running shoes, and a turtleneck. Her only accessory, if you can call it that, is a baseball cap with a picture of a collie on it.

The Thomas family is about ten times more complicated than mine. For starters, Kristy has three brothers: one younger (David Michael) and two older. (Remember Sam? He's one of them. The other is named Charlie.) For years, Kristy's mom handled that family on her own, since Kristy's dad ran out on them a long time ago. Then, Mrs. Thomas met and married this really nice guy who happens to be super-rich. His name is Watson Brewer. When Kristy gained a stepdad, she also gained a few other things. For example, a new home. A mansion (really!) across town. Plus, two new younger siblings: a stepbrother named Andrew, and a stepsister named Karen. And eventually Kristy also gained an adopted little sister named Emily Michelle. She's from Vietnam, and is totally adorable. And after Emily Michelle arrived, Kristy's grandmother moved in to help out. Add the pets (Shannon the puppy, Boo-Boo the cat, and two goldfish), and you have a very full house!

Now that you've met President Kristy, guess who the *vice*-president of the club is? My best friend, that's who. Claudia is vice-president mainly because she's the only one of us who has a private phone line. We could never tie up any of our parents' phones the way we tie up hers. Her duties include (officially) answering the phone during non-meeting times, and (unofficially) supplying junk food to keep everyone munching away when we *are* having meetings.

The treasurer of the club is yours truly, Stacey McGill. I keep track of how much everyone earns, just so we have a record of that. I also collect dues every Monday, which does not make me the most popular person in the room at that time. I practically have to *wrestle* the money away from the other members, even though it's not much. And then I have to make sure we have enough for the things we need (such as payments to Kristy's brother Charlie for driving her to meetings) before we spend any money on luxuries (such as pizza parties). One other thing we use treasury money for is to buy supplies for our Kid-Kits. What are Kid-Kits? They're another of Kristy's great ideas. They are boxes full of games, toys, art supplies and books that we can bring on jobs. Most of the stuff is just old hand-me-downs that we don't use anymore, but the kids love to open those boxes and rummage through them.

The club's secretary is Mary Anne Spier, who happens to be Kristy's best friend. As secretary, she keeps our club record book up-to-date with information on our clients. She also knows all our schedules, and can tell at a moment's notice which of us is free for a job. Mary Anne is as shy and quiet as Kristy is bold, but for some reason they get along really well. Mary Anne has brown hair and eyes, just like Kristy, but she's a little more fashion-conscious. In fact, she recently shocked the rest of us by having a makeover! She got her hair cut in this really cute, short 'do, and even bought new makeup and clothes. We needed awhile to get used to it, but now we think she looks great.

I was surprised that Mary Anne's father let her get a makeover, since he's always been strict with her. He raised Mary Anne by himself (her mom died when Mary Anne was just a baby) and he kept his "little girl" in braids and jumpers for quite awhile. But by now I guess he's realized that Mary Anne isn't his little girl anymore. She's a teenager, and she wants to be treated like one.

Mary Anne is the only member of our club with a steady boyfriend. That may seem odd, since she's so shy and quiet. But Mary Anne is also very sensitive and caring, and *very* romantic, so I guess it makes sense that Logan (that's her boyfriend's name: Logan Bruno) is crazy about her. In any case, Mary Anne is likable, which also explains why she has not one, but two best friends. And guess what? Her other best friend just happens to be her stepsister.

Dawn Schafer, Mary Anne's stepsister, is the club's alternate officer. That means she can take over any job if one of the other officers can't come to a meeting. Dawn has striking looks: long, long pale blonde hair, huge blue eyes, and a casual style of dressing all her own. Her skin just has this healthy glow, which probably is partly due to the fact that she's a vegetarian and a health-food nut. She's the only other person in the club, besides me, who turns down Claudia's offers of Pringles and Devil Dogs. Instead, she'll happily munch on an apple or some trail mix.

Now, Dawn and Mary Anne weren't always stepsisters. That happened pretty recently. Here's how: Dawn grew up in California, but her mother had grown up in Stoneybrook. And when Dawn's parents got a divorce, Mrs. Schafer decided to take her two children (Dawn and her younger brother Jeff) back to her hometown. Not long after Dawn arrived in Stoneybrook, she met Mary Anne and made friends with her and the other members of the club. She and Mary Anne quickly became *best* friends, and soon they discovered something very interesting about their parents. Back in ancient times, when Mary Anne's dad and Dawn's mom were in high school (where they were known as Sharon and Richard), they used to date!

Mary Anne and Dawn helped their parents get re-acquainted, and eventually Sharon and Richard were an item again. Before long, they were married, and Mary Anne and her dad moved into the old (and possibly haunted) farmhouse that Dawn and her mom had been living in. By that time, Dawn's younger brother had moved back to California to live with his dad. He just never adjusted to life in Connecticut. We're sorry for Dawn, because she misses Jeff a lot, but we sure are glad *she* made the adjustment.

There's one more set of best friends in the BSC: Jessi Ramsey and Mallory Pike, our junior officers. We call them that because they are eleven and in the sixth grade and they're not allowed to sit at night, except for their own families. They take a lot of afternoon jobs, though, which is great for them and frees the rest of us up for evening jobs.

Jessi and Mallory have a lot in common.

They both love to read, especially any book about horses. They both look forward to being older and treated less like children by their families. And they are both terrific sitters.

But, like all best friends, they have their differences, too. Jessi is black, with beautiful dark eyes and skin. She's a ballet dancer — a really good one — and she has legs that go on forever. She has a little sister named Becca and a baby brother called Squirt (his real name is John Philip), and her Aunt Cecelia lives with the family.

Mallory is white and has curly red hair, glasses (she'd give anything for contacts), and braces. They're the clear kind of braces, so you hardly notice them, but Mal can't wait to get them off. The Pike family is so big they could form a team for just about any sport: there are *eight* kids! Mallory's the oldest, and in age order after her are Adam, Byron, and Jordan (they're triplets), Vanessa, Nicky, Margo, and Claire. Oh, and there's also Frodo. He's a hamster.

Mal wants to be an author and illustrator of children's books when she grows up. She loves to write. In fact, I think she may be the only member of the BSC who truly enjoys writing in the club notebook, which is another of Kristy's ideas. We each write in the notebook after every job, and then everyone else reads our notes. The information we pass along about our clients is very helpful. I'll admit that, even though I don't love all the extra work. I think it makes us better sitters.

The BSC also has two associate members, who don't often attend meetings but who *do* take on sitting jobs when we're overbooked. Shannon Kilbourne, a girl from Kristy's new neighborhood, is one of them. She's been coming to meetings more than she used to lately (although she wasn't there that day because of a dentist appointment), and we've enjoyed having some "new blood" in the club. Shannon is pretty, with thick, curly blonde hair, high cheekbones, and deep blue eyes. The other associate member is Logan Bruno, Mary Anne's boyfriend. A lot of people don't think boys can be good baby-sitters, but Logan is great. He doesn't come to meetings too often, maybe because he feels outnumbered by us girls.

Anyway, now that you know just about everything there is to know about the club, let me tell you about our meeting that day. It was a busy one.

Kristy called the meeting to order as soon as the clock said five-thirty. "Any business?" she asked.

"Well, it's dues day," I said.

"Tuesday?" said Claudia with a grin. "Sta-

21

cey, it's not Tuesday, it's Monday."

"No, *dues* day," I repeated.

"You need new shoes?" asked Kristy.

"No, *dues*."

"You've got the blues?" asked Dawn, giggling.

I put my hands on my hips. "You *guys!*" I said. They all laughed and handed over their money, and I stuck it into the manila envelope we use for a treasury.

"Any other business?" asked Kristy after we had answered a few phone calls and set up some jobs.

"I think I may have another client for us," said Mary Anne. "I was talking to this new girl in my gym class. She hates gym as much as I do. Anyway, she has a little brother named Georgie, and she said her mom may need a sitter for him sometimes. She's a really nice girl. Her name's Tasha Hoyt."

I gasped. "Did you say Hoyt?" I asked. I glanced at Claudia. "I think I met her brother today. Does she have a twin?"

Mary Anne nodded. "His name's Terry."

"Right," I said softly, almost to myself. Already I knew more about the new boy. He was a twin!

"Okay," said Kristy. "It's always good to keep an eye out for new clients. Nice work, Mary Anne."

Mallory cleared her throat. "I have some business," she said shyly. "It doesn't really have to do with baby-sitting directly, but it could affect us."

"Yes?" asked Kristy.

"Well," said Mal, "did anybody else read that article in the paper last night? The one about counterfeiters in Stoneybrook?"

"Counterfeiters?" I said. "Here? That's ridiculous. Why would counterfeiters come to little old Stoneybrook?"

"It's true," broke in Dawn. "I read the article. It said they may be here *because* Stoneybrook is so little. There's just a small police force here, and the bank tellers and shop clerks might not be very sophisticated, so the counterfeiters can pass their bills more easily."

"Wow!" I said. "What if one of our clients gave us a fake bill? How would we tell?"

"The article said fake money is hard to spot sometimes," said Mal. "There's new technology that makes it easier for people to counterfeit. But a lot of times the money *feels* different, and there are some little things you can watch for, like whether the money has tiny red and blue lines in it or not."

"Real money does," said Dawn, "and fake money doesn't."

"So what if you get a fake bill and try to use it?" asked Mary Anne.

"You can get in a lot of trouble," replied Dawn. "Plus, you don't get to keep the money. The government confiscates it. But I don't think we have to worry too much. They said it's mostly big bills, like twenties and fifties, that are being passed."

Just then, the phone rang. I grabbed it. "Hello?" I said. "Baby-sitters Club." And as soon as the person on the other end started to talk, I forgot about the mystery money.

"This is Janice Hoyt," said the woman. Terry's mom! I almost jumped out of my seat. "My family is new in town, but our neighbors told us we would find a reliable sitter at this number. I need one for my son Georgie, on Saturday night."

"Sure," I said as soon as I caught my breath. I took her number and told her we'd call her back as soon as we checked our schedule. I was hoping I'd get the job, just so I could get a peek at Terry's house, but it turned out I was already booked for an all-day job on Saturday. Kristy ended up taking the job, and soon after that call our meeting was over.

Claud grabbed me just before I left her room that afternoon and whispered to me, "Wear your red dress tomorrow. Terry won't be able to resist you in that!"

I grinned at her. It sure was fun to have a new boy in school.

CHAPTER 3

"Hello, Stacey," said Dr. Johanssen, opening the door to let me in. "Charlotte is so excited about your plans for today. She's talked about nothing else all week."

It was Saturday morning, and I had arrived at the Johanssens' a little early for my sitting job. I guess I was looking forward to the day almost as much as Charlotte was. Charlotte, I should tell you, is one of my favorite kids to sit for. She's eight years old and really smart; in fact, she skipped a grade in school. She loves to read, play with her dog Carrot, and solve mysteries.

Sometimes I almost feel as if Charlotte is the little sister I never had. And I guess she thinks of me as an older sister. She's an only child, just like me, so in some ways we're a perfect match.

Anyway, we had big plans for our day. Dr. and Mr. Johanssen had been invited to an afternoon wedding in Stamford, and they'd be gone until evening. They had offered to drop Charlotte and me off in downtown Stoneybrook on their way out of town, and we were going to spend the whole day there. We planned to eat lunch at a restaurant and shop at the downtown stores. At the end of the day, we'd get a ride home from my mom, who works at Bellair's Department Store as a buyer.

"Stacey!" Charlotte ran down the stairs. "Guess what? I have four dollars and seventy-nine cents to spend today!"

"Wow!" I said. "You're rich, aren't you? And you look like a million dollars, too." Charlotte had gotten dressed up for our day out, in a pink skirt and a white, frilly blouse. I was glad I had also dressed up a little. I was wearing my favorite white miniskirt with a new blue-and-white-striped sweater.

Dr. Johanssen drove us downtown and slipped me some money to pay for our lunch. "Have fun, girls!" she said.

Soon, Charlotte and I were strolling down Main Street, swinging our pocketbooks and stopping every few steps to look into store windows. "This is fun," said Charlotte, grinning up at me. I had to agree with her. It was a sunny day, but it was pleasant and cool. The streets were full of people. And we could spend the whole day together. For the first time all week, I wasn't thinking about Terry Hoyt — I was just thinking about having a good time with Charlotte.

"Look at that picnic basket," said Charlotte, pointing to a fully equipped basket in the window of a housewares store. Blue-and-white checked napkins, pretty blue plates, and white mugs went with it. "Do you think I could buy that?"

"Not with four dollars and seventy-nine cents," I said. "It is pretty, though."

"It would be perfect for a teddy bear picnic," said Charlotte longingly. Then we moved on to the next store, which was Polly's Fine Candy. In the window was a beautiful gingerbread house, decorated with gumdrops and lollipops and swirls of icing. "Yum," said Charlotte, licking her lips.

"Are you hungry?" I asked. "How about heading to Renwick's for lunch?"

Charlotte nodded happily, and we walked around the corner to Renwick's. It's not a fancy restaurant, but it's a fun place to eat. There are red leather booths to sit at, and the waitresses are really nice. "How are you today?" asked the one who brought us our menus. "Our special today is a grilled chicken sandwich, but your little sister might want to look at the children's menu." She smiled at me and left.

"She thinks we're sisters!" whispered Charlotte delightedly.

"Let's pretend we are, just for today," I whispered back.

Charlotte chose an item from the children's menu: the Lucy special, which was a cheeseburger and fries. All the children's items were named after characters from Peanuts. I almost ordered the Linus special myself, which was a grilled cheese sandwich, but at the last minute I decided on a tuna sandwich instead.

Charlotte enjoyed eating lunch in a "real restaurant." She insisted on ordering for herself, and she watched the waitress closely to see how she took down our order. She looked at the other customers. She played with the sugar packets on the table. And she behaved like a lady, saying "please" and "thank you" and wiping her mouth carefully with a napkin after every bite. I could tell that eating at Renwick's was a special experience for her. In fact, she was so excited that she didn't eat more than a few french fries and a couple of bites of her cheeseburger.

After lunch, we headed for Bellair's. Stoneybrook only has one big department store, which was a little hard for me to get used to after living in New York. And Bellair's isn't exactly Bloomingdale's, if you know what I mean. But it's a nice store. We headed straight for my mother's office.

"Well, hello, girls," said Mom when we walked in. "Having a nice day?"

"Definitely," said Charlotte, beaming. "Stacey even let me get apple pie for dessert at Renwick's."

It was true. I had decided that this was a special day, so it didn't matter if she had dessert even though she'd hardly eaten any lunch.

"What's new in the store?" I asked my mother. She's always up-to-date on what Bellair's is carrying.

"Look at these blouses," Mom said, showing me a sketch. "We don't have them yet, but I just ordered them and they'll be here in a month. Aren't they cute?"

I looked at the picture. The blouses were styled like cowgirl shirts, with embroidery on the yokes. "I love them," I said. "I bet Claudia will want one, too."

After we left my mother's office, we headed for the toy department. Charlotte poked around for a long time, trying to decide what to spend her money on. Most of the things she saw were too expensive, but finally she found a troll doll that she said was just what she wanted. She took it to the cash register and paid for it, proudly telling the clerk that she was using her own money.

"Can we go on the escalator now?" she asked, after she'd tucked away her change. Bellair's has an escalator, which is nothing too special to me after all the stores in New York. But kids in Stoneybrook think it's the coolest thing they ever saw, as if it were a ride in an amusement park. That's how excited they get about it.

"Sure," I said. "I'd love to look at the accessories department." We rode up together — and then down and up one more time before Charlotte was satisfied. Then we strolled through the accessories area, looking at barrettes and scarves and socks. I don't know about you, but I *love* accessories. I can never have too many of them. I browsed until Charlotte grew impatient. "One more thing," I told her. "I just want to look at the hair ornaments." She followed me to that counter, and we both saw a beaded headband at the same time.

"Ooh, that's beautiful," Charlotte said as I picked it up. "That would look perfect in your hair."

I tried it on and looked in the little mirror that stood on the counter. "It's nice," I said.

I checked the price tag. "Eight ninety-nine," I said out loud.

"Wow!" said Charlotte. "That's expensive."

I guess anything over four dollars and seventy-nine cents seemed expensive to her, but the price sounded okay to me.

"That looks lovely on you," said the clerk behind the counter.

I looked up and recognized the woman who had spoken. "Oh, hi, Mrs. Hemphill," I said. "Charlotte and I are on a shopping spree today." Mrs. Hemphill knows my mother, and she's also friends with the Johanssens. "I think I'll take it," I said, pulling the headband off. "If I have enough money, that is." I checked my wallet. I had a twenty and a few ones. I pulled the twenty out and looked at it. "I'm sure this isn't counterfeit," I joked.

Charlotte giggled. "I read about that in the paper," she said.

Mrs. Hemphill smiled and took the bill. "I think they're making too much of that," she said. She gave me back a ten and some change and put the headband in a bag. " 'Bye now," she said. "Have a fun afternoon."

Charlotte and I waved and headed out of the store.

The next stop was the the Merry-Go-Round, a store near Bellair's. "I just want to see if they have any new earrings," I said to Charlotte. Claudia and I buy earrings at the Merry-Go-Round all the time. In fact, my favorite pair, which has fish dangling from beaded wires, is from there.

"Hi, Betty," I said to the clerk as we walked in. I've gotten to know her, since Claud and I shop there so often.

"Hi, Stacey," she said. "I didn't know you had a little sister!"

I smiled down at Charlotte, and she grinned up at me. "This is Charlotte Johanssen," I said. "I'm baby-sitting for her. She's my little sister for the day."

"Maybe she'd like a pair of these stick-on earrings," Betty said, handing them over the counter.

"Oh, they're so cute," said Charlotte, looking at the tiny pink hearts. "And they match my skirt. But I don't have very much money left."

"Consider them a gift from me," Betty said, smiling. "Here, I'll show you how to put them on." She came out from behind the counter and knelt down in front of Charlotte.

I walked over to the spinner rack to check out the pierced earrings. I had been looking for a pair to go with my purple jumpsuit. Right away, I saw some that looked just right. They were big purple button-shaped earrings with zigzags of pink on them. I held them up to my ears and looked in the mirror. "These are great," I said. I checked the price. Four ninety-five. No problem. I pulled out my wallet and walked back to the counter.

"How do these look?" asked Charlotte, showing me her stick-ons.

"Terrific!" I said. "Very real. I hope your mother doesn't think I let you get your ears pierced today."

Charlotte giggled and blushed. "I feel grown-up in these," she said. "Maybe I'll ask my mom if I can get more, so I can wear them to school."

Betty smiled at me. "Uh-oh," she said. "I've started something."

I showed her the earrings I wanted and gave her the ten-dollar bill.

Betty took it and turned to the cash register. Then I saw her shoulders stiffen. She turned back to me and gave me a funny look. Then she looked again at the bill. She rubbed it with her fingers. She held it up to the light. "Stacey," she said in an odd voice. "I think this bill is counterfeit."

Charlotte gasped. So did I. "You're kidding," I said.

"I wish I were," replied Betty. "But I'm not. My boss is really worried about taking in counterfeit money, and he's spent a lot of time training us to identify it. I think this bill is fake."

"It can't be," I said. "I just got it from Bellair's!"

"Counterfeit money can be anywhere," said Betty. "I'm afraid I'm going to have to call the police."

"The police?" repeated Charlotte, looking scared all of a sudden. "Are they going to arrest Stacey?"

I was wondering the same thing.

"They'll just want to ask you a lot of questions," said Betty. "Don't worry." She picked up the phone and dialed.

I felt like running out of the store. But Betty must have read my mind. "You have to wait here until they come," she said. "I'm really sorry, Stacey. It'll be okay."

Charlotte and I paced around the store, waiting. I was feeling a little dizzy and very nervous. Charlotte was obviously terrified. She kept asking me questions about what the police would do, but I couldn't answer any of them.

Finally, two young-looking police officers showed up. One of them had a black mustache, and the other had red hair. Betty introduced me to them, and the red-haired one started to ask me questions about where the bill had come from. The other one examined it closely with a magnifying glass. "It's fake, all right," he said, looking up with a frown.

Charlotte looked as if she were about to cry. I heard her sniff a couple of times.

"Can you get the clerk at Bellair's on the phone for me, please?" the red-haired officer asked Betty. "I'm going to have to ask all of you to come down to the station to answer a few more questions."

Charlotte began to wail.

CHAPTER 4

"You *can't* arrest Stacey!" cried Charlotte. "You *can't*! She didn't do anything wrong." She pulled on the officer's sleeve, trying desperately to make him listen to her.

"Charlotte," I said. "He's not *arresting* me." Then I glanced at him. "Are you?" Suddenly I wasn't so sure.

"Of course not," he said. "At least, not right this minute."

I gulped, but then I noticed that he was grinning. Charlotte didn't see his smile, though, and she started to cry even louder. "If Stacey's getting arrested, so am I," she wailed through her tears. "Take me, too!" she said to the officer, sticking out her wrists as though she expected him to put handcuffs on her.

He looked at me and raised his eyebrows. "I think she's been watching too much TV," he said jokingly.

"Charlotte, don't be so dramatic," I whispered, trying to be patient. "They're not arresting me, I promise. And there's no reason for you to come down to the station." I turned to the officer. "Can I call my mom over at Bellair's?" I asked. "She works there, and maybe she can watch Charlotte while I come to the station." The man nodded, and Betty let me use the phone behind the counter.

About thirty seconds later, my mom ran into the Merry-Go-Round. She looked pretty upset. Seeing her made *me* suddenly realize just how upset I was, too. "Mommy!" I said, running into her arms. I hardly ever call her that, but just then I felt like a little kid who needed comfort.

She held me tight. "It'll be okay," she murmured into my hair. "Now, what's this all about?" she asked the officers.

"Just following routine procedure, ma'am," said the one with the mustache. "A counterfeit bill was passed by this young lady," he pointed at me, "and while we don't consider her the perpetrator, we do need to question her and the clerks who served her at both stores she visited."

"I understand," said my mother, nodding. "Well, Stacey, I suppose you'd better go with them. I'll take Charlotte to the store with me, and later on I'll take her back to her house

37

and tell her parents what happened." She held out her hand to Charlotte.

"No!" said Charlotte. "I won't let Stacey go to prison alone!" She grabbed my hand and held it tightly.

This time I almost had to fight back a giggle, even though I was feeling so nervous. Or maybe it was *because* I was nervous that I felt such an urge to laugh. You know how that is, don't you? Sometimes you feel like laughing at the *worst* moments, just because you don't know what else to do. "Charlotte," I said to her. "I promise I'm not going to prison. I'm just going to talk to the officers and tell them what happened. I'll call you later, as soon as I get home." I knelt to give her a hug. "You go on with my mom," I said. "She'll take good care of you."

My mother gave me a quick squeeze, and Charlotte finally allowed herself to be led away. As she walked next to my mom, she kept looking over her shoulder at me, giving me these tragic glances. I had the feeling she was already trying to figure out how to bake a file into a cake, so that I'd be able to break out of jail.

By that time, Mrs. Hemphill had arrived at the Merry-Go-Round, and Betty had told her what was going on. "I just can't believe this,"

Mrs. Hemphill kept saying. "In all my days — "

"Why don't we go to the station," said the officer with the mustache, interrupting her. "There are some people down there waiting to hear your story."

Mrs. Hemphill looked a little indignant. "Well, I never," she said. She followed along as we left the store, whispering to Betty about how the police *used* to have such good manners.

Two police cars were parked outside the Merry-Go-Round. I headed for one, along with Betty and the red-haired officer, and Mrs. Hemphill went toward the other.

"Well, this is an adventure," said Betty, as we sat in the back seat of the cruiser, looking at the wire screen that separated us from the front seat.

"Do you think we're going to get in trouble?" I asked quietly. What I really meant was, Do you think *I'm* going to get in trouble? Betty hadn't done anything but identify the fake bill. I was the one who had tried to pass it. And hadn't Dawn said a person could get into a lot of trouble for doing that?

"Don't worry," said the officer from the front seat. "This is no big deal, I promise you. The worst that'll happen is that you'll get bored to death telling your story fifty times."

I blushed. I hadn't intended for the officer to hear my question. But I felt reassured by his answer. Betty reached over and patted my arm. "I'm sure he's right," she said. "Everybody knows it wasn't your fault."

I gulped. "I hope that's true," I replied. I knew I didn't look like a counterfeiter, but I also knew that a lot of people don't trust teenagers. In some stores in the mall, kids are watched really closely, as if the storeowners think they're going to shoplift or something. That's not something I've been tempted to do, so I've always hated being looked at that way. And now I was being taken to the police station for questioning. Even though the officers had told me I wasn't under suspicion, I felt as if I'd done something wrong. And all I'd done was go shopping! I wasn't sure I'd ever feel the same way about shopping again.

We rode through the streets toward the police station. I was sure that people were staring at us as we drove by, wondering why a young girl like me would be sitting in the back of a police cruiser. I scooched down in my seat, hoping we wouldn't pass by anybody I knew. At least the officer hadn't turned the siren on, and as far as I knew the blue light on top wasn't going around and around.

The Merry-Go-Round isn't far from the police station, but the ride seemed to last forever. Finally, both cars pulled up behind the station, and the officers led us inside. We walked past the desk where the receptionist sits, down a hall, and into a small, stuffy room. A long table was in the middle of the room, with chairs around it. It looked exactly like the rooms in cop movies, the rooms where they question criminals and try to force them to confess. I tried to think of what my confession would sound like. "I did it," I would say. "I admit everything. First I bought the headband and then I bought the earrings. Put me away for life, if you must!" Once again, I felt those giggles coming on.

The officers left Betty and Mrs. Hemphill and me alone in the room, telling us that some other officers would be in to see us soon. As they left, the door slammed shut behind them with a boom. I wondered whether I would find it locked if I tried to open it. Luckily, I didn't have to wonder long. About two seconds later the door opened, and five people walked in. Three were police officers — not "ours," but different ones — in uniform. One of them was a woman. Then there was a man in a regular suit and a woman in a dress. I guessed they were plainclothes police.

They introduced themselves, but I wasn't really listening. I was feeling nervous and dizzy, and the small room seemed very, very full. But then they started to ask questions, and right away I felt better. Answering questions was something I could do. And all the officers seemed very nice. They didn't shout, or shine bright lights on us, or threaten us. They just asked simple questions about what had happened.

Mrs. Hemphill spoke first. She told how I had come into the store, and how pleased she'd been to see Charlotte and me. She went on for quite a while about what a nice young lady I was, and how, while *other* teenagers are often rude and sullen, I was always pleasant and polite. I saw some of the officers exchanging looks as she rambled on, and the woman in the dress jumped in to get her back on track.

"Can you tell us about the actual purchase?" she asked Mrs. Hemphill. And Mrs. Hemphill told her, in great detail, how I had found the beaded headband and liked it so much (*and* how "darling" it looked on me) and paid for it with a twenty-dollar bill. She told them how we'd joked about the bill being counterfeit. And then she told them about the change she gave me.

"The bill seemed fine to me," she said. "I didn't notice a thing wrong with it. Of course, if I *had*, I never would have given it to Stacey."

I was next. I told the same story, except from

my point of view. The officers interrupted me more than once, to check on details. First they asked about where my twenty-dollar bill had come from originally. I couldn't figure out why that mattered, but I told them that I'd gotten it from a client. Then they asked about the ten that Mrs. Hemphill had given me, and whether I'd noticed that it felt different. I hadn't, of course, and told them so. I showed them the headband I'd bought, along with the receipt. Then I told them what had happened in the Merry-Go-Round. When I mentioned the earrings I had decided to buy, I suddenly realized I'd never gotten them.

"What happens to that ten-dollar bill, anyway?" I asked. "I mean, I know you have to confiscate it, but do I get reimbursed?"

The plainclothesman shook his head. "I'm sorry," he said. "But this is just the way the system works. Sometimes innocent people lose out a little."

I was sorry to hear that, but I sure was glad to hear him use the word "innocent." That meant that they believed my story.

After I'd finished, Betty told her story. " . . . and then," she said, when she got to the part about my handing over the ten-dollar bill, "she gave me the money and I noticed right away that something was strange about it. It just didn't *feel* right."

"Good work," said one of the uniformed police officers. "If only everyone was on the ball like that, we'd catch these guys in no time."

Betty flushed a little and looked proud. "Well, my boss trained us," she said. "It's not so hard if you know what you're looking for."

We had finished telling our stories, so I figured the officers would let us go. I couldn't wait to get out of that stuffy room. But they surprised me.

"Okay," said the plainclothesman. "Now that we've got the basics down, we need to go back over all of this information to see if it checks out. Then, after we do that, we have to ask you a few more questions about what you saw in the stores today."

I leaned back into my chair. Apparently we'd be stuck there for a while longer. The police started over again with Mrs. Hemphill, reading back her story (they'd been taking notes) and questioning her on every detail. She seemed to enjoy the attention, and went on and on until I felt my eyelids start to droop.

Then the officers came back to me. They asked me again about the contents of my wallet when I had started out that day. They made me go over and over the exchange of the twenty for the ten and change. They even made me count out my change to make sure it had been correct. "We just need to be absolutely sure that the bill in question did come from the cash register at Bellair's," explained the woman in the dress, in a gentle tone. I think she could see that I was becoming impatient with all the questions.

Betty spoke next. I could tell she was tired of telling about her amazing skills as a counterfeit bill detector. She sounded less proud and more bored every time she went over the details.

"All right, then," said the plainclothesman. He seemed to be in charge of the questioning. "Next, we need to ask what each of you saw in the stores this afternoon. Any strange people? Anybody who looked suspicious, for any reason at all? Did anything unusual happen, anything out of your normal routine?" This last question was directed at Mrs. Hemphill.

By this time, even Mrs. Hemphill seemed bored with talking. Still, she managed to dredge up memories of the customers she had helped that morning. She got fired up again and started to talk in great detail about a mother pushing a stroller with twins in it, a young man looking for a birthday present for his girlfriend, and an elderly woman who wanted a "new look."

I expected the officers to break in at any moment and ask her to cut it short, but they didn't. They seemed to want every last detail. I tuned out a little bit and started to think about my own memories of being in Bellair's. When the officers began to question me, I was ready. "I saw a man with a hat on," I remembered. "That seemed strange, since the weather is kind of warm, and anyway he was indoors. I also saw Mr. Fiske, my English teacher, but I didn't say hello to him because I felt kind of shy. And I saw a woman carrying seven shopping bags. I remember, because I counted. I was amazed that anybody could do so much shopping in one day."

I was sure that nothing I told them was relevant to the case, but they listened closely anyway, and took notes. Then they turned to Betty again, and then they asked us all to go back one more time and see if we could come up with anything else. I was too exhausted to think by then, but Mrs. Hemphill couldn't resist adding one more detail about the young mother's outfit. Then, finally, the officers thanked us and let us go.

All I wanted to do when I got home was flop down on my bed and sleep for awhile. I was so tired out from all that questioning that I could hardly find the energy to tell my mom what had happened. But I did, and then I dialed the Johanssens' number and spoke to Charlotte. She had calmed down by that time, but she still sounded relieved to know I wasn't spending the night behind bars.

When I finished with Charlotte, I was feeling more energetic. I decided to call my friends and tell them about my adventure. And by the time I'd finished talking to all of them, including Kristy, who was sitting at the Hoyts' that night, we had decided to get together the next day, just so we could discuss my adventure together. This was the most exciting thing to happen in the BSC for quite awhile!

CHAPTER 5

Saturday

    I just adore sitting for new clients. It's fun to get to know a new family and to learn about the kids. Each kid is so different, and I love finding out who they are and what they like to do. The Hoyts seem like a nice family, although they're not easy to get to know. Mr. Hoyt seems a little strict, and all the kids are shy. But I'm glad they moved to Stoneybrook, and I hope we'll be sitting for Georgie often.

Kristy was looking forward to her job at the Hoyts'. She loves to be the first sitter for a new client. In fact, I think she feels that, as president, she *should* be the first BSC member to meet new clients. "I see myself as the representative, of the club," she once told me. "I think the clients are impressed that the president of the BSC will be their first sitter. And also, I feel a responsibility to check out new clients so we can be sure they're okay."

Personally, I don't think it matters which of us sits first, but these things are important to Kristy.

"Watson told me to come inside with you when we get there," Charlie said to Kristy as he drove her to the Hoyts'. "Since you don't really know this family or anything."

Kristy nodded. "Okay," she replied. "I guess he's right."

It's important to know your clients when you're baby-sitting. Most of our clients are regulars, so this isn't usually a problem. But when the clients are new in town, we always ask someone to come to the door with us the first time, just to get a sense of what the family is like.

Charlie pulled up in front of a tidy red house. "Thirty-five Reilly Lane," he said. "I guess this is it." He and Kristy stepped out of the car and walked to the front door. Kristy rang the bell.

A girl answered it. A pretty girl with long, shiny brown hair in a braid down her back. Kristy noticed right away, she told me later, that this girl had gorgeous hazel eyes. "You must be Kristy," the girl said, smiling shyly.

"Yup," replied Kristy. "Are you Tasha?"

The girl nodded. Then she looked at Charlie and raised her eyebrows. "Is this your boyfriend?" she asked Kristy.

"Oh, no!" exclaimed Kristy. "I'd never bring my boyfriend on a job. I mean, if I even *had* a boyfriend." She blushed, thinking of this boy Bart she kind of likes. "This is my brother, Charlie. He just came to the door with me because — I mean, since I don't know your family — I mean, he came to — "

"To check us out?" asked Tasha.

"Well, yes," said Kristy.

Charlie had been staring at Tasha. Obviously he thought she was something special. Now *he* blushed. "Uh, well," he started to say.

Just then Mr. and Mrs. Hoyt came into the room, and Tasha introduced everyone.

"Nice to meet you, Kristy," said Mrs. Hoyt. "I've heard such good things about your baby-sitting club."

"Thank you," replied Kristy.

Mr. Hoyt checked his watch. "We're going to be late for the concert if we don't get started soon," he said. "All ready to go, Tasha?"

Kristy turned to Charlie as the Hoyts were talking, and nodded toward the door. She was trying to let him know that she felt fine about the Hoyts and that he should leave. But Charlie was still staring at Tasha. Finally Kristy nudged him with her elbow. "Don't you have to be going?" she asked him.

"Oh, right. Well, have fun at your concert," he said to Tasha.

"Thanks," she said. "I'm looking forward to it. Especially since Dad is coming. He usually misses these things because of his job."

"Tasha!" said her father sharply. "Please go tell Terry and Georgie that we're going."

Tasha headed upstairs, and Charlie said his good-byes and left. Mrs. Hoyt took Kristy into the kitchen and showed her where she'd left important information for Kristy. "It's not often that Mr. Hoyt and I get to go out with the twins," she said, "so this is a special event. We'll probably stop for some dessert afterwards, but we won't be too late."

"That's fine," said Kristy.

"Oh, here's Georgie," said Mrs. Hoyt.

Kristy turned around and saw a little boy with familiar-looking brown hair and hazel eyes. He wore big, horn-rimmed glasses, and he was very skinny. She figured he was about seven years old. "Hi, Georgie," she said. "I'm Kristy. How are you?"

"Fine," he answered shyly.

"I have a little brother who's seven. I wonder if you're in his grade?" she said.

"I'm seven and a half," Georgie replied, very seriously.

"Maybe you're in the same class as my brother," Kristy went on. "His name is David Michael."

Georgie shook his head. "I don't really know anybody here yet," he said.

Mrs. Hoyt was bustling around getting food out of the refrigerator. "Here's some salad you two can eat," she said, "and some leftover lasagna. I'll just put this in the oven to heat up, and then we'd better be off."

Kristy met Terry as the Hoyts were leaving. She told me later that she thought he was really cute, but not her type. "Too shy," she said. "He barely said hello to me, even though I tried to be friendly."

Soon Kristy and Georgie were sitting down to dinner together at the kitchen table. Kristy decided Georgie was one of the quietest kids she'd ever met. She decided to find out about his interests. "So," she said. "Do you like to play softball?" She was wondering if she should ask him to join the Krushers, the team she coaches.

"I love it!" he said, looking enthusiastic for the first time.

"Great. There's this team you could probably join, if you'd like to."

His face closed up again. "I'm not allowed to play on teams," he said. "Dad says they take up too much time and that I'm better off at home doing my homework and stuff."

Kristy raised her eyebrows. That seemed a little strict to her. She took a few more bites of lasagna and searched for another topic of conversation. "How long have you been wearing glasses?" she finally asked.

"I got them about a year ago," Georgie said. "One day I was walking along and I thought I saw a big goose standing by our mailbox. It turned out to be a huge white rock. That's when I knew I needed glasses."

"Oh," said Kristy. "Where were you living then?"

"In Iowa," he said. "No — in Oregon. Sometimes I get mixed up."

"Has your family moved a lot?" Kristy asked.

Georgie nodded. Then he shook his head. "Not that much," he said. "Can I have some more salad?"

Kristy thought for a second that he felt uncomfortable with the subject and was trying to change it. But that seemed silly. "Sure," she said, passing the bowl. "Do you like to read?" she asked.

"Oh, yes! Want to see all my books?"

They cleared the table and cleaned up the kitchen, and then Georgie led Kristy upstairs to his room. Kristy noticed moving boxes piled in the hallways, and when she reached Georgie's room she found that most of his books were still packed away, too. He opened a carton and started to rummage through it.

"How long has your family lived here?" Kristy asked. It seemed as if the Hoyts hadn't unpacked much beyond the bare necessities.

Georgie thought for a moment. "About three weeks," he said.

Three weeks? And they still weren't unpacked? The Hoyts must be a busy family.

Georgie pulled out a book. "This is my favorite," he said. "Tintin. I have twelve Tintin books." He settled down to look at it, leaning against his bed. Kristy sat down next to him with one of the other Tintin books, and they spent some time reading quietly.

After awhile, Kristy closed her book. "Hey, your mother told me she left some brownies for us," she said. "Want to go downstairs and get some?"

"Sure," Georgie replied, putting down his book.

Back in the kitchen, Kristy found the brownies and poured two glasses of milk. Then she and Georgie headed for the family room. It was full of boxes, too, but there was a comfortable couch. They sat down to eat brownies and watch TV. "Do you have a VCR?" Kristy asked, thinking that she could bring over a movie the next time she baby-sat.

Georgie shook his head. "Dad never wants to join at the video stores. He says it's too expensive and that movies are a waste of time, anyway."

Kristy thought Mr. Hoyt sounded more and more strict all the time. But Georgie didn't seem to miss having a VCR. He watched *Wheel of Fortune* happily, munching on his brownies. Then, just as a guest was about to win a ton of money, the phone rang.

Kristy jumped up and ran to the kitchen to answer it, thinking it might be Mrs. Hoyt checking in. But it was me, calling to tell her what had happened that afternoon. "Wow!" said Kristy. "So there really are counterfeiters in Stoneybrook." I gave her the details about my ordeal at the police station. Kristy was spellbound. Then, suddenly, she heard a cry from the family room.

"Kristy!" called Georgie. "I spilled my milk!"

"Gotta go," Kristy told me. She hung up and looked around for a mop. There wasn't one in sight, so she opened the door to the basement. No mop hanging there, either. She ran down the hall to a closet she'd noticed before, and was just about to open it when Georgie darted out of the family room.

"No!" he said. "Don't open that."

Kristy stared at him. "I can't open this closet?" she asked, not quite understanding.

"Right," he said. "It's — it's full of stuff," he said lamely. "It might fall out."

"Well, okay," replied Kristy. "But I'm trying to find a mop. Do you know where one is?"

"It's all right," said Georgie. "It's just a little puddle. Most of it already got soaked into the couch. We can use paper towels."

Kristy sighed. She knew that the Hoyts wouldn't be crazy about milk soaking into their couch, but there wasn't much she could do about it now. They cleaned up the mess together, and by then it was time for Georgie to get ready for bed.

He changed into his pajamas and climbed into bed, and Kristy read him a story out of one of his Tintin books. Soon his eyelids were drooping. "Kristy?" he said sleepily, just as she was closing the book.

"Yes, Georgie?"

"I think I like Stoneybrook," said Georgie. "And you're a nice baby-sitter."

Kristy smiled. "Thanks. Now go to sleep, okay?" She tiptoed to the door and switched off the light. His breathing became deep and regular before she had even left the room.

Kristy headed downstairs. She couldn't resist calling me, to hear more details about my day. I told her everything as quickly as I could, knowing we shouldn't tie up the Hoyts' line. It was then that we decided the BSC should meet the next day, just to talk some more.

After Kristy hung up, she wandered around the house tidying up a little. There was a little desk in a corner of the living room, and she noticed some papers on the floor underneath it, so she bent to pick them up. "I wasn't snooping, I swear," she told me later. But she was surprised and confused by what she saw when she reached for the last envelope. Sticking out of it was a photo ID from a junior high in Oregon. The picture on it looked just like Tasha, but the name beneath the face read "Tina Harris" instead of Tasha Hoyt. Kristy stuffed it back into the envelope, threw it on the desk, and tried to forget about it. After all, it was none of her business. Was it? Anyway, she was too interested in me and my day at the police station to spend much time thinking about the Hoyts.

CHAPTER 6

"But I didn't do it!" I cried. "I'm innocent, I swear!" I didn't even know what I'd been accused of, but it was clearly something terrible. A man in a black uniform was marching me down a long, dark hallway, and I was wearing handcuffs and leg chains.

I saw faces staring at me as I was led past the many windows that were set into the walls. Claudia, looking very sad. My math teacher, Mr. Zizmore, looking puzzled. Charlotte, with tears rolling down her face.

"I want to talk to a lawyer," I said. "I want to talk to my mommy!"

But the man just kept marching, and soon we were standing in front of a huge steel door. He pushed a button and the door swung open. We walked through it, and it slammed shut behind us with an awful bang that seemed to echo forever. The next hallway was even darker than the first, and there were no windows and no faces to be seen. Then we walked through another door, and another, and another. Each one slammed shut behind us with a bang that sounded very final. *Bang, bang, bang*, went the doors. I was never going to get out of that awful place. *Bang, bang, bang!*

"Stacey, wake up!" my mother said, shaking me. "I've been knocking on your door for the last five minutes."

I sat up with a start. "You mean it was all just a dream?" I asked. "Oh, Mom!" I threw my arms around her.

"Did you have a nightmare, hon?" My mother patted my back. "Well, it's all right now. Except for the fact that it's almost ten-thirty. Weren't you planning to go to Claudia's this morning for a meeting?"

"Oh, my lord!" I said. "Is it really that late?" I'd had trouble falling asleep the night before, mainly because I kept thinking about that scene at the police station. But once I finally fell asleep, I must have slept like a log. I rubbed my eyes and stretched, trying to get used to the idea that I wasn't going to rot in some dungeon after all. Aren't nightmares the worst? Especially the ones that feel so real.

I got up and dressed quickly. Then I headed downstairs, gulped down some toast and juice, and set out for Claudia's house. We'd agreed to meet there at eleven.

When I arrived, everyone else was already there. Claudia was sitting on her bed, still wearing her tie-dyed pajamas. Mary Anne and Dawn sat on either side of her. Kristy was in her usual spot in the director's chair, but for once she didn't have a pencil tucked over her ear. Since this wasn't a regular BSC meeting, I guess she didn't feel she was going to need it. Shannon sat cross-legged on the floor, and next to her were Jessi and Mal.

I had heard them all talking as I ran up the stairs, but when I came in they suddenly stopped. Everyone looked up at me expectantly. "Uh, hi, guys," I said, not knowing what else to say.

"Morning, Stace," said Claudia. "How's our counterfeiter today?" She grinned.

I frowned. "I'm not a counterfeiter," I protested.

"We know," said Kristy, giving Claud a Look. "But I sure hope our clients don't hear about this."

"What do you mean?" I asked.

"Well, I've been thinking about it," she said. "This could hurt the club's reputation if it got out. That one of us was passing fake bills, I mean."

I started to say something, but Kristy held up her hand. "I know you didn't do it on

60

purpose. We all know that. But you know how rumors can spread, right?"

I felt terrible. How did I get into this mess? All I did was try to buy a stupid pair of earrings. Suddenly I hated those earrings. How could I have ever thought they were pretty? "I'm sorry," I said miserably.

"Don't be sorry," said Mary Anne. She looked upset. She can't stand to see anybody unhappy. "It's not your fault, and I think Kristy's being kind of mean."

"I agree that it's not Stacey's fault," said Dawn. "But I think Kristy has a point. Our clients have to trust us completely, and if they have any doubts it may hurt our business."

The room was quiet for a moment. Then Jessi spoke up. "You know what this reminds me of?" she said. "That time with Mrs. Gardella's ring."

"Oh, no!" said Claud, putting her hand over her mouth. "You're right! And that was poor Stacey, too. First she gets accused of being a thief, and now she gets dragged down to the police station for questioning in a counterfeiting case!"

I hung my head. Somehow I'd forgotten about that business with the Gardellas. It didn't seem fair that these things kept happening to *me*. Jessi and Claud were talking about this time not too long ago when I was sitting for a new client. The morning after my job, the client had called to say that her diamond ring was missing. She basically accused me of stealing it! Of course, I hadn't. Fortunately, we managed to straighten out the mess.

"That was different, though," said Mallory thoughtfully. "I mean, Mrs. Gardella was threatening to tell all our other clients that Stacey was a thief. This time, who's going to tell?"

"Well, Dr. Johanssen knows about it," said Kristy.

"She'd never spread gossip about something like this!" I said.

"No way!" Claud agreed.

"What about Mrs. Hemphill?" asked Dawn.

We just looked at each other. Everybody knows that Mrs. Hemphill loves to talk. The story was probably all over Stoneybrook by now.

"Oh, no," I groaned.

"Okay, look," said Kristy. "We know Stacey didn't do anything wrong. But who knows what other people might think? We have to take action. I hearby move that we do everything we can to solve this mystery."

"Yea!" said Mallory with a huge smile. "I

was hoping you'd say that. I, personally, am so excited to know that there are counterfeiters in Stoneybrook. I mean, I'm sorry you got mixed up in this, Stacey, but isn't it just like a Nancy Drew book or something?"

"Exactly," said Claud. "I know what you mean. I've been dying to figure out a way to catch these crooks." She reached under her pillow and pulled out some red licorice. "Anybody want some? Suddenly I feel hungry." She pulled off a strip and passed the package around.

"But we don't know anything about counterfeiting!" said Shannon. "How are we going to find out who's doing it?"

"We could learn about it," I said. "I bet there's information about it at the library. And anyway, we know a little bit, don't we?"

"Sure," said Kristy, absently taking a bite out of a licorice strip. "Ugh," she added, "it's too early in the day for junk food." She put it down. "I mean, we know that these people are printing money, right? So they have to have some kind of printing press, and they must need supplies for it."

"So we find out where they sell printing supplies, and stake out the place!" Mallory said.

"Also, we have to keep our eyes out for

people who are suddenly spending lots of money. I mean, like, gobs of cash," said Dawn.

"So maybe we should stake out the Cadillac dealership," said Jessi. "Isn't that the first thing crooks do? Buy a flashy car?"

"Hmm . . ." said Dawn. "I was thinking more about just hanging out at the mall and checking out who's buying jewelry and stuff." Jessi's face fell. "But a car place is probably a good idea, too," Dawn added quickly.

"Maybe we should stake out banks," said Shannon. "To see if anyone is making big deposits."

"Don't you think a crook would just keep it under his mattress or something?" I asked.

"Well, maybe," she admitted. "But you never know."

"Stacey," Mary Anne said, "what did that bill *feel* like, anyway? I mean, I want to know it if I have a fake bill."

"I swear I couldn't tell the difference," I said. "It seemed fine to me, or else I wouldn't have tried to use it."

"But you said Betty could tell right away," said Dawn.

"I know," I replied. "She said it felt too smooth. Regular bills are engraved, and you can feel the ink on them. But my bill was just flat."

Kristy reached into her pocket. "Maybe we should all check our money," she said. She took out a ten-dollar bill and some ones, put her nose up to them, and stared at them closely. "They seem fine to me," she said.

Soon, everyone had pulled out their wallets and dug around in their purses. We were passing money around, rubbing it between our fingers, and examining it with a magnifying glass that Claud keeps in her desk drawer. "These all seem fine," said Dawn. "Hey, Stace, maybe you should check out the treasury!"

I nodded. "Good idea," I said. "But I don't have it with me, since this isn't a regular meeting. I'll check it as soon as I get home."

I think some of my friends were almost hoping to find counterfeit bills, just because they thought it would be exciting. But I never wanted to see another fake bill as long as I lived. I was glad when Kristy announced that all our money seemed okay.

While we were sorting out whose money was whose, the phone rang. Kristy answered it, listened, and handed it to me. "For you, Stacey," she said.

"Hello?" I asked.

"Hi, Stacey. This is Charlotte. I called your house, but your mommy said you were over at Claudia's."

"Hi, Charlotte," I said. "How are you?"

"I'm fine, except that I'm worried about you. Are you still going to be able to baby-sit for me?"

"Sure!" I said. "Why wouldn't I?"

"I thought maybe because you got arrested, you wouldn't be allowed to baby-sit anymore."

"Charlotte," I said, trying not to sound impatient, "I told you, I wasn't arrested. Please stop worrying. The police questioned me, but now that's all over, and I'm fine."

"Okay," she said in a small voice. She didn't sound convinced.

"I have to go, Char," I said gently. "I'll see you soon, okay?"

" 'Bye, Stacey."

I hung up the phone and sighed. "I wish Charlotte hadn't seen the police come. This has really upset her."

"She'll be all right," said Kristy. "Hey, speaking of Charlotte, I wonder if she'd be a good friend for Georgie Hoyt. He seems kind of lonely, and she lives near him." She told us about her sitting job at the Hoyts'. I listened, hoping to hear more about Terry.

He and I had talked a few times at school that week, but I hadn't exactly gotten to know him yet. He had learned my name, and he smiled shyly and said, "Hi, Stacey," when he passed me in the hall, but that was about it. Kristy didn't seem to have any new information, and I didn't want to ask her about him. Claudia was the only one who knew about my crush so far, and I wanted to keep it that way.

Our "nonmeeting" ended soon after that. We had decided to break up into teams to do research on counterfeiting that week, but I wasn't really looking forward to it. I mean, I *did* want to see those criminals caught, but part of me also just wanted to forget about counterfeit money.

When I got home that afternoon, my mom told me that someone had called for me. "I know," I said. "Charlotte, right? She called me at Claudia's."

"No, it was a boy," answered my mother. She smiled at me. "He didn't leave a message, but he did say he'd call back."

I wondered who it could be. Sam hadn't been calling me too often, since we'd talked about seeing other people. In fact, I had heard through the grapevine that he had been calling up this girl in his grade named Kathy. Calling her *and* dating her. I knew it was what we had decided to do, but I still felt jealous and hurt. So when the phone rang half an hour later, I answered it in my frostiest voice.

"Is that you, Stacey?" asked the boy on the other end. "This is Terry Hoyt."

I managed not to gasp out loud. "Oh, hi!" I said. "How are you?"

"I'm fine. Um, listen, I was wondering — " He paused, and then seemed to gather up his courage. "Would you like to go to the movies with me on Friday?"

I automatically thought for just a second about Sam, and whether dating Terry would be disloyal to him. But in the next second I remembered Sam and Kathy, and I blurted out, "Yes, I'd love to!" We talked for awhile longer, about school mostly, and then we said good-bye. I hung up the phone and leaned back on the couch, thinking about those gorgeous hazel eyes.

CHAPTER 7

At first, when we had talked about it in Claudia's room, I hadn't been all that interested in researching counterfeiting. But by lunchtime on Monday, I was totally psyched for it. Why? Well, first of all because I had another horrible nightmare on Sunday night. In this one I was being questioned by a mean-looking police officer. Bright lights were shining in my face, and he kept saying, over and over again, "You knew it wasn't real. You knew it wasn't real." He was shaking a ten-dollar bill in my face.

Then, on top of that, when I reached school I found out that the story of my experience with the fake money had spread quickly. I found out about *that* when Cokie Mason came up to me in the hall after social studies. "Trying to pass fake bills, I hear," she said. Cokie is *not* one of my favorite people. "I thought you and your friends made plenty of

69

money. I guess your baby-sitting business must be falling off."

I was so mad I couldn't say a thing. But I decided then and there that I would catch those counterfeiters no matter what it took. In fact, I decided to go along with each of the teams my friends had formed, and do all the research I could.

I headed for the lunchroom and found my friends sitting at their usual table. Terry Hoyt was sitting across the room, but I hardly glanced at him. I was on a mission. "Hi, you guys," I said, putting my tray down next to Claudia. I glanced at my food and realized that I wasn't hungry at all. (If I had been, I would have been in trouble, since the "beef stew" looked like something you might clean out of the bottom of a drain.) I glanced at Kristy and Mary Anne. "Are you almost done?" I asked them. "Let's hit the library." They were one of the teams, and they had planned to check out the school library to see what they could find.

"Whoa, you're in a hurry, aren't you?" asked Kristy. "We just sat down."

I could hardly eat, since I was so eager to get started, but because of my diabetes I had to eat *something*. I finished off my salad and a roll, and then I just sat and stared at Kristy and Mary Anne, which I think made them nervous. They gulped down their food. Then Mary Anne sighed and said, "Well, we might as well get going."

When we reached the library, we fanned out in different directions. Mary Anne went to the card catalog. Kristy hit the encyclopedias. And I just paced nervously. Finally, the librarian asked me if she could help me find something.

"Oh, uh, well," I said. "I'm trying to learn how to make counterfeit money."

She gave me a strange look.

"I mean — " I said, blushing, "not for myself. I want to find out how *other* people do it. You know, criminals."

She nodded. "Well," she said, "you might try the encyclopedia."

I pointed to Kristy. "That's what she's doing," I said. "And my other friend," I pointed to Mary Anne, "is checking to see if you have any books on the subject."

"Good idea," the librarian said. "Then I suppose the next thing would be to check on whether there have been any recent newspaper or magazine articles on the topic."

I nodded. "There *have* been some," I said, "at least in the newspaper. How do I get copies of those?"

She showed me how to use the newspaper index to find out the dates of the articles. Then she went into a closet and found the actual newspapers, and showed me how to make copies of the ones I wanted. I copied three articles, including one from that morning that mentioned a "local teenager" who had been questioned regarding a counterfeit bill. I read that one quickly. Then I ran over to Kristy. "Look!" I said, showing it to her. "That's *me*, isn't it?"

She looked it over and nodded. "They don't mention your name, though. That's good."

I put the copies into my notebook, after folding them carefully. "There isn't really any new information in these," I said, "but it's good background stuff. Have you found anything?"

"Not much," Kristy admitted. "These encyclopedias are kind of out of date. But I took some notes on the history of counterfeit money."

Mary Anne joined us. "They don't have any books on counterfeiting," she said. "Just books about coin collecting."

I looked over at three boys who were standing by the dictionaries, whispering and laughing. "There's Alan Gray," I said. "Do you think he's doing the same thing we are?" No way did I want Alan Gray, the most obnoxious boy in school, to crack this case before we did.

"They're probably just looking up dirty words," said Kristy. "Good way to waste a lunch hour." She looked disgusted.

Just then, the bell rang. "Shoot," I said. "Time to get back to class. And we've hardly found anything."

"That's okay," said Kristy. "We're just getting started. It may take awhile."

I knew she was right, but I was feeling impatient. The sooner we got rid of these counterfeiters, the better. I went to my classes, but I couldn't concentrate, not even in math. Luckily, Mr. Zizmore didn't seem to notice. Usually I'm his favorite student, since I actually enjoy math problems, but that day I couldn't have told you what X equaled if my life depended on it.

After school, I made quick plans with Dawn and Claudia. They were going to pick me up at the Stoneybrook Public Library on their way downtown to do *their* research at the police station. While I waited for them, I would work with Jessi and Mal in the reference room. I was hoping we'd have better luck there than Kristy and Mary Anne and I had had at school.

"Don't forget to ask my mom for help," said Claudia. "She knows everything about that place."

Jessi and Mal were waiting for me when I arrived at the library. They had already checked the card catalog and found one book that might have a chapter or two on our subject. Jessi went looking for the book, and Mal and I sat at a table, planning our next move. Then Mrs. Kishi came over to see us.

"Hi, girls," she said, in a normal tone of voice. I guess she doesn't have to whisper in the library, since she's in charge of it. "Stacey," she went on, "I was sorry to hear about your trouble on Saturday."

I didn't know what to say. Mallory jumped in. "We're trying to find out about counterfeiting," she said. "Where can we look?"

"Well, for the most up-to-date information," replied Mrs. Kishi, "you can try the periodical guide." She led us to a shelf of green books and showed us how to look up our subject. "Make a list of the magazines you want," she said, "and one of the clerks will find them for you."

Mal and I got to work, and soon Jessi sat down next to us with a book in her hand. She started to page through it while Mal and I looked up "counterfeiting" in the indexes Mrs. Kishi had shown us. Soon we had quite a list. Mallory took it to the desk, and a few minutes later a stack of magazines sat in front of us.

We learned some interesting things from those articles. For example, the paper that money is made out of is from a "secret recipe." These tiny blue and red fibers run through it, and it's almost impossible to make paper that looks the same. Also, we found out about all the ways people try to make money. Some people take a one-dollar bill and bleach out the parts that say "1" or "One." Then they copy them on a fancy color copying machine, after making them look like twenty-dollar bills, or other big bills. That kind of fake is pretty easy to spot, though.

Meanwhile, Jessi had set aside the book, after marking a few pages to copy later. She was leafing through some of the magazine articles and she showed me one of them. "Look at this," she said. "It says that because of the new kinds of color copying machines, it's easier to make phony money. Before, you had to know how to do engraving, and photography, and all kinds of stuff. But now all you need is a good copier."

"That's true," said Mallory, "but it says here that the Secret Service is already figuring out new ways to make money harder to copy on those machines. They're putting in special threads and strips that can only be seen when you hold up the bill to light. If a bill doesn't have them, it's fake."

"Check this out," I said, showing my friends the article I was reading. "It says that passing counterfeit money is a felony! I'm lucky I'm not in jail right now."

"You're not in jail," said Jessi, "but somebody else should be. I hope we can catch him. Or her."

We read for awhile longer. I have to admit that learning about counterfeiting was pretty interesting. Some of the people who have done it were real artists who spent their lives figuring out the best way to copy money. Others were just crooks who did it the easiest way possible. Also, I found out something I'd never thought of, which is that some people make counterfeit *coins*. You wouldn't think you could get rich making fake pennies, but I guess if you made enough of them, you could.

Some of the stuff we learned made me a little nervous, too. For instance, how serious a crime it is to make or pass counterfeit money. I mean, one entire branch of the Secret Service spends all their time going after counterfeiters.

Jessi and Mal and I took the articles we'd found, plus the book Jessi had discovered, to the copy machine to make copies. "Let's try something," said Jessi, pulling a dollar bill out of her pocket and putting it onto the machine.

"No way!" I said. "Are you nuts? I mean, *I* know you're just fooling around, and *Mal* knows, but if you got caught copying that — " I blew out some air and rolled my eyes.

Jessi put the bill back in her pocket. "Sorry," she said. "You're right. I don't know what I was thinking. I guess I just wanted to see what it would look like, even though this isn't a color copier."

At that moment, Claudia and Dawn showed up, ready to head for the police station. I left Jessi and Mal to finish the copying and the three of us rode downtown on our bikes. "Do you guys have a plan?" I asked them.

"Not really," said Dawn. "We're just going to ask for whoever's in charge of this case, and see if they'll give us more information about what kind of bills are being passed and stuff."

We walked into the police station, still breathing hard from our ride. Dawn led us to a desk where a police officer was sitting. He looked up. "Well," he said, "if it isn't Nancy Drew herself." He grinned at Dawn. "Caught any more dog-nappers lately?"

Dawn blushed, but she looked kind of flattered. I realized that the officer must be the one she'd dealt with not long ago, when she was trying to track down these people who were stealing dogs in the Stoneybrook area. At first the officer hadn't paid much attention to her, but when she actually cracked the case, he admitted that she was a pretty good detective. We — the members of the BSC — even got our pictures in the paper then!

"We're interested in that counterfeiting

case," she said. "Can you tell us who's in charge of it?"

"I can tell you, but you won't get anything out of him," said the officer. "This is big stuff. We're not talking about a missing Pekingese or something, you know."

Dawn nodded. "I know. But we thought — "

"Tell you what," the man said. "There's no way the sergeant will talk to you. But I can give you one of these fliers," (he rummaged around on his desk), "that we passed out to the local merchants. That'll give you some information." He lifted up a pile of papers, then put it back down. "Huh," he said. "Guess we're out of them. Oh well. Listen, I think you're better off just staying out of this one, anyway. These guys are serious criminals. You don't want to get mixed up with them." He winked at us, smiled, and went back to his work. We had no choice but to leave.

"Dead end," said Dawn as we left the building.

"Not really," replied Claudia. "I bet we can get hold of one of those fliers. Let's go see Betty at the Merry-Go-Round."

"Great idea," I said. I knew I could probably also get one from my mom, but maybe it was just as well that she didn't know I was playing detective.

When we reached the Merry-Go-Round, Betty was waiting on a customer. She smiled at us, but she looked busy. We dawdled around for a few minutes, looking at earrings and hair accessories — Claud even picked out a scarf that she wanted to buy — until Betty was free.

"Oh, Stacey," she said, stepping out from behind the counter. "I'm glad to see you. I felt so bad about what happened the other day."

"It's okay," I told her. "It wasn't your fault. You did the right thing."

"I guess so. "But who would have thought they would grill us like that? I needed a long, hot bath when I got home, I can tell you."

We talked for awhile about our experience at the police station, and about how my friends and I were hoping to help catch the criminals, and then I asked her about the flier. Betty went back behind the counter and pulled a piece of paper out of a drawer. "This is it," she said. "You can have this one. It's extra."

I gave it a quick look. The heading said *Merchants Are the First Line of Defense*, and it told what to do if a customer gives you a fake bill. "This is interesting," I said. "Thanks."

Betty smiled. "Sure. Good luck catching those guys. And whatever you do, don't tell Mrs. Hemphill what you're up to. She'll broadcast it all over town by tomorrow morning."

I laughed and put the flier into my notebook, along with the copies I'd made at the school library. I had learned a lot that day, and I was beginning to get an idea of what the BSC was up against. It wasn't going to be easy, but I thought we were on the way to cracking the case. Maybe I would be able to sleep through the night soon, without having nightmares.

CHAPTER 8

Wednesday

Boy, if I was one of those counterfeiters, I'd really be scared. Not only is the entire BSC on the case, but there are also two little junior detectives doing everything they can. Becca is having fun, but Charlotte is really serious. Stacey, you have a big fan in Charlotte — but I guess you knew that.

"**A**ll right, mesdemoiselles, show me your finest second position," said Jessi. She was talking to her little sister Becca and Charlotte, who happens to be Becca's best friend. Jessi was sitting for them that afternoon, and they were playing "Ballet Class." Jessi was imitating her teacher, Mme Noelle, while Charlotte and Becca pretended to be grown-up ballet students. The two of them stood at Jessi's practice *barre* and stretched their necks so that they looked elegant. They turned out their feet and made what they thought were graceful gestures with their arms.

"Magnifique!" said Jessi. "Miss Romsey, please show me an *arabesque.*" (Miss Romsey is what Mme Noelle always calls Jessi. That's how she pronounces Ramsey.) Becca put her arms over her head and stood on tiptoe. "Excellent!" said Jessi. She looked at Charlotte and noticed that she didn't seem to be paying attention anymore. Instead, she was making faces in the mirror.

First she would smile, grinning as widely as she could. Then she would frown until she looked as if she were about to burst into tears. Next, she'd grimace, trying to look as mean as possible. Jessi watched, smiling to herself, until Charlotte caught her eye in the mirror and blushed bright pink. "Sorry!" Charlotte said. "What position are we supposed to be in?"

"It doesn't matter," replied Jessi. "It's just a game." She giggled, remembering a time when Mme Noelle had caught her doing the same thing during a particularly boring class. Mme Noelle had been furious, but she'd forgiven Jessi soon afterward, when Jessi performed a perfect *tour jeté*. (That's a type of graceful jump.)

"It's about time to get going, anyway," said Jessi. "That is, if you guys still want to go to that workshop at the library."

"I do!" said Becca.

"Me, too," said Charlotte. "It sounds like fun."

There was a special program in the children's room at the library that afternoon. The kids were going to make birdhouses, and each child would be able to take one home at the end of the afternoon. Jessi's Aunt Cecelia had offered to drive them to the library and pick them up at the end of the program.

When they reached the library, the children's room was packed with kids. It was a mob scene. Four tables were set up with materials for the birdhouses: old milk jugs and cartons, big plastic soda bottles, gourds, and paint for the finished projects. About thirty kids were milling around, waiting for the program to start. Jessi settled Charlotte and Becca at one of the tables and then sat down in a reading corner nearby.

Presently Becca began working on a gourd birdhouse, and Char began working with a milk carton. The children's librarian was giving directions in a loud voice, while kids traded seats, started fights, giggled and shrieked, and spilled paint all over the tables.

Soon the kids settled into their projects, though, and the room became a tiny bit quieter. Jessi wandered over to the new book display and looked at the titles. She saw a book called *Horses of the World*, and took it back to her spot where she leafed through it, looking at the pictures and fantasizing about owning a white stallion that could run as fast as the wind.

"Jessi?" Jessi looked up to see Charlotte standing in front of her.

"Are you done already?" asked Jessi. "Let's see your birdhouse."

"I'm not done," said Charlotte. "I can't concentrate on it."

"What do you mean?"

"I just keep thinking about Stacey getting arrested," said Charlotte. She looked upset.

"But Stacey's okay. She wasn't really arrested, you know. The police let her go."

"What if they come after her again?" asked

Charlotte. "Stacey isn't a criminal, but they don't know that. They might put her in jail."

"I don't think they will," said Jessi, trying to sound comforting. "Anyway, the BSC is working on the case. Before you know it, those counterfeiters will be caught."

Charlotte's eyes lit up. That was all Jessi had to say. Charlotte forgot about her birdhouse and sat down next to Jessi, eager to talk about the mystery of the counterfeiters.

"You're working on the case?" she asked. "What have you been doing? Can I help?" Charlotte loves mysteries, and she has proven to be a pretty good detective in the past.

Jessi started to tell Charlotte about some of the research she and Mallory and I had done. "Counterfeiting is serious business," she warned. "I don't think it's a good idea for you to get mixed up in this. Your mother might not like it." But Charlotte kept asking questions and Jessi couldn't resist telling her what we'd learned.

"I can't believe they can just make money on copy machines!" Charlotte said when Jessi had finished.

"Copy machines?" asked Becca, who had wandered over to join them.

"Counterfeiters use them," explained Charlotte. Jessi noticed a gleam in her eye. "I bet if we staked out some of the copy machines around here, we could catch those crooks."

Jessi looked doubtful. She didn't really think that counterfeiters would use public machines to do their business. "I don't think — " she began, but Charlotte and Becca interrupted her.

"Can we?" asked Charlotte. "We could go to all the copy machines in town and watch for awhile. Please, Jessi?"

"Please?" Becca chimed in.

"What about your projects?" Jessi asked, pointing to the paint-covered tables.

"We already have a birdhouse in our yard," said Charlotte. "Being detectives would be much more interesting."

Becca agreed. "It's too noisy here, anyway," she said.

Jessi thought for a minute. If they were bored with their projects, she didn't want to force them to stay. And even though they were unlikely to catch any counterfeiters in the act, spying on copy machines seemed like a harmless way to pass the rest of the afternoon. "Well, all right," she said.

"Yea!" said Becca.

"Yea!" said Charlotte. "We're going to clear Stacey's name."

Jessi told the children's librarian they were leaving, and the three of them headed upstairs.

"There's a copy machine here, isn't there?" whispered Charlotte as they passed through the reference room.

Jessi nodded, remembering how she had almost copied money on that very machine. She led the girls to it. "It's not a color copier," she said, "so probably they wouldn't use this one."

"Let's watch for a few minutes anyway," said Charlotte. "Just for practice."

They sat down on the stairs near the machine and waited to see who would use it. The first person was a skinny high-school boy with glasses. He copied a few pages from a magazine. Next was a woman with two little blonde girls, who copied some kind of form. Then came an old man who copied an article out of a newspaper. Nobody copied any money.

"Ready to go?" asked Jessi, after the man had finished and walked away.

"Okay," said Charlotte. "I think our next stop should be the stationery store. They have a copier there, and also we can buy a little notebook to make spy notes in."

Jessi smiled. Who knew? Maybe Char would come up with some ideas that the BSC hadn't thought of. They trooped off to the stationery store.

"This one will be just right," said Charlotte

firmly. She had picked out a little black notebook with lined paper. "It looks like a spy notebook."

"Can I choose the pen?" begged Becca. She looked through the selection carefully until she spotted a purple felt-tip that seemed perfect to her.

Jessi paid for the selections, and then the three of them found the spot where the copy machine was.

"You pretend to be looking at birthday cards," Charlotte instructed Jessi. "I'll check out the wrapping paper, and Becca, you act like you're choosing ribbon." She was getting a little bossy, but Jessi decided to follow her orders. The three of them loitered in that section, waiting for someone to come and use the copier.

"Jessi," Charlotte hissed. "Come here!" She waved her over. Jessi joined her by the wrapping paper.

"What is it, Char?" she asked.

"Remember when Stacey was being questioned at the police station?" Charlotte asked. "Didn't they ask her about suspicious people?"

Jessi thought over what I'd told her and nodded. "They wanted her to try to think of everyone she'd seen in the store that day."

"Well, what did she tell them?" asked Charlotte. "I mean, we should be looking out for those same people, shouldn't we?"

Jessi shrugged. "I guess you're right," she said. "Let me think. I know she mentioned a man wearing a hat indoors — "

"Hold on a second," said Charlotte, getting out the notebook and the pen. "Let me write this down." She started to make notes. "Okay, man with hat. Who else?"

"A woman with lots of shopping bags," said Jessi. "I remember that."

"Good, good," said Charlotte, writing fast. "Anybody else?"

Jessi thought for a minute. "Oh, I know," she said. "She saw Mr. Fiske, her English teacher. I know who he is, because he once came to my class to make a special presentation. He has blond hair and a mustache."

"Great," said Charlotte, still taking notes. "Is that all?"

"I think so," said Jessi.

Just then, Becca made a hissing sound, and they turned to look at her. She pointed to the copy machine. A man with a briefcase had begun to copy a whole bunch of papers. He looked as if he were in a hurry.

Charlotte's eyes lit up. "He's not wearing a hat, but he looks suspicious," she whispered to Jessi. She began to scribble frantically in the notebook. Jessi looked over her shoulder and saw that she was writing down a complete description of the man, from the color of his suit to the initials monogrammed on his briefcase.

Meanwhile, Becca was edging closer and closer to the machine, trying to get a look at what the man was copying. Soon she was standing right next to him. He gave her an annoyed look. "Are you waiting for the machine, little girl?" he asked.

Becca shook her head and backed up a little, but she was still peering at his papers.

"Why don't you run along, then?" he said. He glanced at Jessi, clearly expecting her to take charge.

"Becca," said Jessi. "Time to go!" They ran out of the store, giggling nervously.

"He was just copying all these boring papers with writing all over them," said Becca. "I didn't really think he was making money, but I wanted to practice my spying."

The three of them hit three more places: a copy shop, the copier at the town hall, and a machine in the lobby of the post office. Charlotte made notes on every person they saw using the machines, but none of them fit the descriptions I had given.

Finally, they went to the office equipment store, where there are copiers for sale. Charlotte made Jessi pretend she was researching copy machines for a school project, and they listened as the clerk told them about the best models for each kind of work. "I can't show you our finest model right now," said the clerk, "because my boss is demonstrating it for a client. But that's it, over there. It does beautiful color reproduction."

Jessi looked at the machine and gasped. Standing next to the huge, complicated copier was none other than Mr. Fiske. She hustled Becca and Charlotte outside as quickly as she could. "I don't believe it," she said, half to herself, after she'd told the girls who the man in the store had been. Could Mr. Fiske really be involved, she wondered? Maybe Charlotte's spying game hadn't been so silly after all. Still, they couldn't just stand there and watch him price fancy copiers. And anyway, it was time to return to the library to meet Aunt Cecelia. Suddenly, Jessi couldn't wait for that afternoon's BSC meeting. She had some interesting information to pass on.

CHAPTER 9

I pulled off the purple sweater and threw it onto the bed. It joined a huge pile of other clothes I had tried on and decided against wearing: a floral sundress (too summery), a red jumpsuit (too flashy), and a pair of bleached-out jeans with bows at the ankles (too casual).

I was having a hard time figuring out what to wear for my date with Terry. On the one hand, I wanted to look really good. I wanted to wear something special, something he hadn't seen me in at school. On the other hand, I knew he was shy, so I didn't want to overwhelm him with anything too outrageous.

After our BSC meeting that afternoon, Claudia and I had had a short discussion about what I should wear. We had decided on the red jumpsuit, but as soon as I tried it on I knew it was all wrong.

I pulled a black sweater-dress out of the

closet and held it up in front of me while I looked in the mirror. It was a little too dressy, I decided, and maybe too hot, too. I checked my watch. Terry was due in fifteen minutes! This was getting ridiculous. I gazed into my closet, hoping that a dress I'd never seen before would appear magically. No such luck.

It's times like these that make me wish I had a sister. Somebody who would help me figure out what to wear. Maybe even someone who would *lend* me something to wear. Once in a while my mom is a big help with this kind of stuff, but for some reason that night I didn't want to ask her.

I made a quick call to Claudia. "Help!" I said. "I'm down to the wire here."

"What about your white sweater and those blue-and-white polkadot leggings?" she asked, after I had explained the situation. "You look great in that outfit, especially when you put that white bow in your hair."

"Perfect," I said. "You saved my life. I forgot all about those leggings." I hung up and dressed quickly. The outfit looked fine — just right for Terry, I thought. I was brushing on some blush when I heard the doorbell ring.

"Stacey!" my mom called a few seconds later. "Terry is here."

I checked my lipgloss one last time and ran down the stairs. "Hi," I said, smiling. Terry looked terrific in a pair of chinos and a tan sweater. He smiled back at me, and I could tell he thought I looked nice, too.

"I guess you met my mom," I said. "But let me introduce you anyway. Mom, this is Terry. Terry, this is my mother, Mrs. McGill."

Terry stuck out his hand. "Terry Hoyt, that is," he said. "Terry James Hoyt. I'm very pleased to meet you."

My mom looked a little surprised, but she shook his hand and told him it was her pleasure. I asked Terry to sit down for a moment, and as he headed for the couch my mom and I exchanged looks behind his back. She raised her eyebrows and smiled at me. I had a pretty good idea what she was thinking. "Polite boy," probably. Guys like that always impress my mom.

The three of us chatted for a few minutes. Mom asked Terry where his family had moved from, and he told her about Portland, Oregon. Then Terry asked Mom about her job, and she told him about Bellair's. I listened politely, but I was glad when Terry finally glanced at his watch and said that we should get going if we were going to catch the movie we had planned to see.

My mom had offered to drive us downtown, and Terry's mother was going to pick us up. We had decided on a new movie about a family that gets marooned on Mars. It was supposed to be a comedy, which is why I wanted to see it, but it also had a lot of science-fiction stuff, which was why Terry thought it would be fun.

My mom dropped us off in front of the movie theater. Terry paid for the tickets, and I bought the popcorn and soda. I like to split the cost when I'm dating, especially if it's a first date. I want the guy to know I'm independent.

We found seats near the front and settled in to watch the show. The movie was funny, but what was even funnier was this man in the audience who kept laughing in this honking, snorting way. I knew Terry thought it was hilarious, too, because he looked at me whenever we heard that laugh. Every time the man cracked up, *we* cracked up. It sounded as if an elephant or something were loose in the theater.

I kept hoping I'd spot the man so I could see what he looked like, but I couldn't find him. I did see Alan Gray with two of his obnoxious friends, and also Mary Anne and Logan. I waved to Mary Anne, but I couldn't tell if she saw me.

Terry didn't try to put his arm around me or anything, but our hands brushed twice when we both reached for popcorn at the same time. I wondered for a second what it would be like to kiss Terry. Then I remembered that I barely knew him. Still, what I did know, I liked.

I have to confess that I didn't pay much attention to that movie.

When it ended, we walked out into the lobby. I spotted Mary Anne, and pulled Terry over to meet her and Logan. "This is Mary Anne Spier," I told Terry. "And Logan Bruno."

Terry stuck out his hand, just like he had done when he'd met my mother. "Terry John Hoyt," he said. "Nice to meet you."

John? I could have sworn he said Terry *James* when he met my mom, but I must have remembered wrong. I mean, the guy knew his own name, right?

"Hi, Terry," said Mary Anne. "I think I've met your sister. She's in my gym class."

"Gym?" asked Terry. "I bet you haven't seen her smile much, then. She hates gym."

"So do I," confessed Mary Anne. "Tasha and I get along great."

"Did you like the movie?" Logan asked.

"Sure," said Terry. "Especially the part where they got stuck in the airlock of the spaceship. That was intense."

Logan and Terry started to talk about the movie, and Mary Anne and I looked at each other and shrugged. I guess she hadn't paid too much attention, either. "You look great," she said.

"Thanks," I answered. "You, too."

"Terry's nice," she whispered. "Cute!"

"I know," I whispered back.

"What are you guys doing now?" she asked.

I checked my watch. We had an hour before Terry's mom would pick us up. "I don't know," I said. "Maybe we'll get a snack somewhere." I turned to Terry. "Are you hungry?" I asked.

"Sure, I'm always hungry."

I told him about the Rosebud Cafe, and we decided to head over there. Mary Anne and Logan said they'd join us for a soda, but they couldn't stay long.

"Hey, this place is cool," said Terry, as we walked into the restaurant. He looked around at the fifties decor. "It reminds me a little of the Hard Rock Cafe."

"You've been to one?" I asked.

"Sure," he said. "When we lived in New York for awhile. I used to go there a lot."

"You lived in New York?" I asked. "Me, too." We found a booth and sat down, and Terry and I talked about New York. Mary Anne asked if Terry had ever been to the top of the Empire State Building. She loves doing touristy things in New York.

The waitress brought us menus, and we ordered. Mary Anne and Logan just asked for Cokes, but Terry ordered a cheeseburger and fries. I ordered the Rosebud Special, which is a turkey sandwich with their secret dressing.

"So, Terry," asked Logan. "Do you play any sports?"

"I like to watch baseball," said Terry, "but I've never played on a team."

"Who do you think will be in the Series?" asked Logan. "I'm rooting for the Yankees."

"I hope the Rangers make it," said Terry. "They've been my favorite team ever since we lived in Texas."

"Boy, you've moved a lot," I said, blurting it out without thinking.

Terry blushed. "Not so much," he said.

I thought for a minute. Portland, Oregon. New York. Texas. And now Stoneybrook. And hadn't Kristy said that Georgie mentioned living in Iowa? That made at least five places, which seemed like a lot to me. But I didn't say anything, since Terry didn't seem to want to talk about it.

Mary Anne leaned over and touched my arm. "You wouldn't believe what Tigger did today," she said. "He was so cute. He found this hair tie of Dawn's, and he was chasing it all over the house." She turned to Terry. "Do you have any pets?" she asked.

"No, we can't," he answered. "I mean —

my brother is allergic," he added quickly.

Terry looked uncomfortable again, so I changed the subject. "How do you like SMS?" I asked.

"Well, it's pretty different from my old school. The last one was just a tiny, country school with about fifty kids in each grade," he said.

Hmmm. I always thought Portland, Oregon, was a pretty good-sized city. Had Terry lived one other place that he hadn't mentioned yet? I decided to change the subject again, since I didn't want him to think I was giving him the third degree.

"Did you guys hear that man at the movies?" I asked. "The one who was laughing so much?"

Terry did a great imitation of that honking laugh, and we all cracked up. In the midst of our giggles, our food arrived. Terry offered his french fries around, and Logan took a few. Mary Anne sipped on her soda, and I dug into my sandwich.

I glanced at Terry as we ate. He was *so* cute. Funny, too. And generous, the way he shared his food. I liked how polite he was, and he seemed really smart. Everything about him was attractive. Still, something was just a little "off" about him. But I shrugged at my doubts. He was a great guy, and I was having a terrific time on our first date. I wasn't in love with him or anything, but he sure was nice.

My thoughts were interrupted when I felt a sharp pain in my ankle. I looked up, surprised, and found Mary Anne giving me a strange look. Had she kicked me under the table? I looked back at her, and she brushed at her chin. Then she gave me another significant look. For a second I was confused, but then I understood. I wiped my own chin and discovered a smear of that secret dressing on it. Oh, my lord! I'd been sitting there with goop all over my face. I glanced at Terry, but he was deep in conversation with Logan. He hadn't noticed. I sighed with relief and gave Mary Anne a grateful look. She smiled back.

Then she turned to Logan. "Don't you think we should be going?" she asked.

Logan hesitated, but Mary Anne pulled on his sleeve and smiled at him. I knew she wanted to leave so Terry and I could have some time alone. Mary Anne is so sensitive that way.

They finished their sodas and left, and for a minute Terry and I just sat there feeling shy. First dates are hard, aren't they? Sometimes you just can't think of a thing to talk about.

"So, where did you live in New York?" I asked finally. Unfortunately, Terry had started to speak at exactly the same time.

"How long have you known Mary Anne?" he asked.

We laughed. "You go first," I said. He talked for awhile about the Greenwich Village neighborhood where he had lived. Then I told him about my friendship with Mary Anne and the other members of the BSC. Soon we had forgotten about being shy. The conversation felt easy and comfortable, and I found myself liking Terry more than ever.

Then, just as Terry was telling me about something funny that Georgie had done, I looked up and the smile froze on my face. The door of the cafe had opened, and Sam was walking in. He wasn't alone.

"What's the matter?" asked Terry.

"Nothing," I said. "Go on."

He continued his story, but I could hardly pay attention. Sam was standing at a booth near ours, talking to a bunch of high-school guys. And next to him, hanging on his arm and smiling up at him, was a pretty red-haired girl. I recognized her from the production of *Peter Pan* that we had been involved in, and I knew she was in high school.

I tried not to feel jealous. After all, Sam and I had agreed to date other people. And anyway, I was at the cafe with Terry. But seeing Sam with someone else gave me a strange feeling. I watched them talk, forgetting to listen to Terry. Then, suddenly, Sam turned and saw me. "Oh, no," I said, under my breath. Quickly, I wiped my chin again — just in case.

Sam and his date walked over to our booth. "Hi, Stacey," he said. "This is Kathy."

"Hi," I said, trying to sound normal. "This is Terry." The situation was right up there with My Most Uncomfortable Moments. The four of us tried to make a little small talk, and then Sam and Kathy headed for the booth in back of ours and sat down.

I noticed that Terry had finished his cheeseburger. I looked down and saw that half of my sandwich was still left, but I had lost my appetite. "Want to get going?" I asked. "We can walk around a little until it's time to meet your mom."

"Sure," said Terry. I think he understood that I felt awkward. We paid the check and left as quickly as possible. "Old boyfriend, huh?" asked Terry, when we were standing outside.

I nodded. "It's no big deal," I said. I put my arm through his and we walked around the block. Being close to Terry made me forget about Sam or any other boy. It had been a wonderful date, and Terry James — John? — Hoyt was definitely major crush material.

CHAPTER 10

"So *then*," I said, "I reach up to touch my chin and find out that I have this gross pink glop all over my face!" It was Monday afternoon, and I was at Claudia's for a BSC meeting. I was sitting on her bed, with Claud and Mary Anne on either side of me. We had gotten a few calls, I had already collected dues, and we had taken care of club business, so I was giving everybody a blow-by-blow description of my date with Terry. By that time, my crush was common knowledge, so I thought I might as well tell all the details.

"Nobody noticed but me," said Mary Anne, meaning the secret dressing on my chin.

"I sure hope not," I said. Just thinking about it made me blush. "Anyway, it was really a nice date. Except for Sam."

"Sam?" asked Kristy. "I haven't heard about that part yet. What happened?"

"Well, maybe you know that he's dating that girl Kathy," I said.

Kristy shook her head. "Sam never tells me anything."

"Take it from me, then," I said. "He's dating that high school girl who was in *Peter Pan* — "

"Kathy?" asked Dawn. "The redhead? She's gorgeous."

"I know," I said. I told my friends how they had come over to our table and how awkward I had felt. "It was like, 'Hi, old boyfriend, meet new boyfriend,' " I said. "Yuck."

"Are you going to go out with Terry again?" asked Shannon.

"I'd like to," I said. "He really is a nice guy. He even called me on Saturday just to say what a good time he'd had the night before. Not too many guys bother to do things like that."

"I thought he was so shy," said Dawn.

"Well, he is and he isn't," I replied. "He just doesn't seem to want to talk about himself too much. Like, he didn't really answer me when I asked what his father did. I only asked because the Hoyts seem to move so much." I paused. "But he *is* friendly," I went on. "He even — "

"What?" asked Dawn, leaning forward. "Did he kiss you?"

I looked at Claud. Of course, I had already told her about it. "He did. When his mom drove me home, he walked me up to the door and kissed me good night. It was just a little kiss, but it was nice."

"Woo, woo," said Kristy. "Wait'll Sam hears about that!"

"You wouldn't!" I cried.

"No, I wouldn't," she admitted. "But I bet it would drive him crazy. Yesterday he was asking me who that 'new kid in your school' is. And now I know why. He's jealous."

Somehow, that made me feel better. I mean, Sam Thomas is not the love of my life or anything, and I think our new arrangement is just fine. But I still feel a little jealous when I see him with another girl, and I was sort of glad to know he felt the same way.

The phone rang then, and Kristy dove for it. "Baby-sitters Club," she said. "We care about kids!" She listened for a moment. "Sure," she said. "We'll call you right back, Dr. Johanssen." She hung up and turned to Mary Anne. "Who's free on Wednesday afternoon?"

Mary Anne checked the record book. "Dawn and Claudia," she said.

"Wednesday?" repeated Dawn. "You know, I was planning to take this cooking course at the natural food store that afternoon.

It's about new ways to cook tofu."

Mary Anne grimaced. "Sounds wonderful," she said. "So, Claudia, how about you?"

"Fine," said Claudia. "I already know all the ways *I* like tofu. On somebody else's plate, for example."

Dawn threw a pillow at her.

Kristy picked up the phone and called Dr. Johanssen back to tell her that Claudia would be Charlotte's sitter. When she hung up, she turned to face us and she looked serious. "Okay," she said. "Now that we've heard about Stacey's date, let's move on to the important stuff. How are we going to catch those counterfeiters?"

Ugh. I wished those dumb counterfeiters had never come to town. But the truth is, all weekend — well, except maybe for that one second during Terry's kiss — I had thought about how we could nab them. I mean, my reputation was at stake. What if Terry found out he was dating a felon? Not that I had actually been arrested or anything, but still. . . . And what about the reputation of the BSC? If Mrs. Hemphill really got talking, we might lose business. Come to think of it, we hadn't received very many calls that afternoon.

"Well, we've done a lot of research," I said. "I have all these articles," I pulled a pile of papers out of my backpack, "and some other notes and stuff." I passed the papers around, and everyone started leafing through them.

"Charlotte sure is interested in the mystery," Jessi said. "You should have seen her spying on people all over town." She told us about Charlotte's detective work.

"So most likely they're using some kind of fancy copy machine," said Shannon, after skimming one of the articles.

"Definitely," I said. "I mean, there's no point in doing it the old-fashioned way anymore. The copy machines make it easy."

"But they make it easy to get caught, too," said Mallory. "The new counterfeit bills aren't as real-looking as the old engraved fake bills. I mean, look how quickly Betty figured out that Stacey's bill wasn't the real thing."

"Don't remind me," I groaned.

"Sorry," said Mal. "All I'm saying is that we shouldn't have any trouble tracking these guys down. All we have to do is stake out copiers. We don't even have to bother watching the Cadillac dealership or jewelry stores or anything like that."

"I'm glad *you're* so confident," I said. "In the meantime, I'll be checking every bill before I spend it. I never want to be in that situation again."

Kristy had been quiet for a few minutes. Suddenly, she spoke up. "Oh, my lord!" she said.

"What?" I asked.

"Is something wrong?" asked Mary Anne, concerned.

"It sure is," said Kristy. "I just figured something out. I think I may know who the counterfeiters are."

"You're kidding!" I exclaimed. "Tell us! Who?"

Kristy paused. "You're not going to like this," she said, looking at me.

"What do you mean?" I asked. "Of course I'll like it, if you really cracked the case."

"I think it may be the Hoyts."

"Oh, come on," I said, laughing a little. "I thought you were serious."

"I am," said Kristy.

There was silence for a moment, and then everyone started talking at once. Everyone but me, that is. I was just sitting there picturing Terry's sweet smile and beautiful eyes. Somebody that cute couldn't be a criminal. I was sure of it.

"I don't understand," Shannon was saying. "Why do you think it's the Hoyts?"

"A lot of reasons," said Kristy. "Everything just fell into place all of a sudden." She held up a hand and started to tick off her fingers, one for each point she made. "First of all, they move around all the time. Second, they haven't even unpacked at their house here, which probably means they're ready to move again at a moment's notice. Third, Georgie won't let me open a hall closet in that house. What could be in there that could be so bad for me to see?" She paused for a second and glanced at me.

I must have looked as if I were in shock. I felt Mary Anne put her arm around me.

"Fourth," Kristy continued, "Terry won't say what his father does and can't even remember all the places he's lived. And fifth," she held up her hand with all five fingers spread. "I found that fake ID of Tasha's. Her picture, with a different name. What else can all of this mean?"

"I — I'm sure there's some explanation for everything," I said.

Nobody jumped in to agree with me. Instead, they all just sat there thinking.

"The Hoyts moved here, what, a few weeks ago?" said Dawn finally. "Isn't that about when the counterfeiting started?"

"Dawn!" I cried. "I can't believe you said that. So *what* if they moved here recently? That's circ — circumfer — circumstantial evidence!" I finally spit out the word, which was one I had heard on that TV show with the judge. Circumstantial evidence is evidence that doesn't necessarily prove anything but that might change a judge's — or a jury's — mind. Sometimes it's not even allowed in court.

"Okay, what about the fact that they haven't unpacked much?" asked Claudia.

I turned to her. My best friend, a traitor. "Maybe they're just very busy," I said coolly.

"What about that closet that Georgie wouldn't let Kristy into?" asked Mal. Everybody was against me. I knew they didn't mean to appear that way, but I also knew I had to stick up for Terry. He and his family just *couldn't* be counterfeiters.

"The Hoyts deserve their privacy, the same as any other family," I said. "Who knows? Maybe the closet was just a big mess and Georgie was embarrassed for anyone to see it."

"That's true," said Mary Anne thoughtfully. "I wouldn't want certain people to see some of the closets in *our* house."

I gave her a grateful look. At least one person in the club didn't automatically assume that the Hoyts were guilty.

"Then again," said Mary Anne, "I did wonder about Terry the other night. He seemed kind of secretive, if you know what I mean."

Oh, great. Even Mary Anne was ready to arrest Terry's family. "You guys," I said. "All of this is totally circumstantial. You haven't said a thing yet that even makes me suspicious." Okay, maybe I was overstating the case. But I did feel that they were jumping the gun.

"All right," said Kristy. "What about that fake ID?"

"Uh," I said, stalling for time. I couldn't think of an answer for that one. "Maybe it wasn't even Tasha's," I said finally. "Maybe it belonged to a cousin or something. A girl that looks just like her."

"Yeah, maybe," said Kristy doubtfully.

"Anyway," I said, "I just don't think it's them. They're a really nice family." I didn't mention my previous thought: that Terry was too cute to be a criminal. Somehow I didn't think that would go over too well.

"They *seem* nice," said Kristy darkly. "But that might be their cover. They move to a town, infiltrate the neighborhood, even let their kids make friends with the locals," here she shot me a significant glance, "and then they start making money. When the situation gets too hot and the police start to sniff them out, they just up and move to the next town."

I was stunned. Did Kristy really think Terry had asked me out because his counterfeiter-father had told him to? "No way!" I cried. Then I calmed down a little. "Look, I just don't

111

think it's a good idea to concentrate on the Hoyts. For one thing, I'm positive they're innocent. And for another thing, there are a lot of other suspicious people we should be watching out for and checking up on."

"That's true," said Kristy. "I mean, if we spend all our time on one set of suspects, another suspect may be getting away with making fake money right under our noses. We're not *positive* it's the Hoyts, so we should keep an eye on all our suspects."

"Who *are* our suspects?" asked Mallory.

"The man wearing a hat indoors, for one," I said. "He really looked strange to me. I haven't been able to forget about him."

"Isn't there anyone a little easier to find?" asked Jessi.

"Well, there's Mr. Fiske," I said slowly. "He was at the store that day, and he was also spotted pricing fancy copiers." I started to talk faster. "Plus, he has access to that copier in the basement at school! I bet he's up to something. He's always seemed a little odd to me."

"Mr. Fiske?" asked Dawn. "Odd? He's the most normal guy in the world."

"Yeah, but those are the ones you have to look out for," I said. "I have a feeling he may be our man." Soon after we finished talking about Mr. Fiske, our meeting ended and we headed home.

I wasn't quite as sure about Mr. Fiske as I sounded, and I was determined to work even harder on finding out who the counterfeiters were. My reputation wasn't the only one at stake now. Terry's was, too.

CHAPTER 11

Wendesdy

Im begining to think that Stasey may be rite about mr. Fisk. I had my susspishions befour, but now Im really starting to wonder. I mean, if hes not contrafeeting, what is he up too? Anyway, as long as Charlotte is on the case, well deffinitly solve it. Shes the best detectiv Ive ever seen.

Claudia knocked on the Johanssens' door. She was on time for her sitting job, but just barely. She had stopped at home after school to pick up some art supplies for a special project she had planned to work on with Charlotte. A large pad of drawing paper was under one arm and a box of paints and Magic Markers was under the other. She had tucked a paintbrush behind one ear, and in order to knock on the door she'd had to hold a bag of crayons in her teeth.

"My!" said Dr. Johanssen, when she answered the door. "You certainly look prepared for — for something."

"Shpeshial art phroject," Claud said, her words muffled by the bag in her mouth.

"Yea!" cried Charlotte, running up behind her mom. "What are we going to make?"

"It'sh a shecret," said Claudia. She took the bag out of her mouth and handed it to Charlotte, along with the pad of paper. "Why don't you set us up in the kitchen while I say goodbye to your mom?"

Charlotte ran off, bag and pad in hand.

"I'll be home by five," said Dr. Johanssen. "I know you have a meeting this afternoon, so I won't be late. Looks like the two of you will be having some fun today!"

"I hope so," said Claudia. She was excited

115

about the idea she'd come up with. She had thought of it during math class. Now, math is my favorite class because I love it, but it's one of Claud's favorite times for daydreaming and creative planning. She may not know how many apples Suzy needs for two and a half pies, but she does come up with some terrific ideas for new projects.

When Claud entered the kitchen, Charlotte was ready to get to work. She had put the drawing pad in the center of the table, and laid out the crayons, arranged by color, next to it. She sat in one of the chairs, looking eager.

Claudia dumped the rest of her supplies on the table. "We don't really need all these colors," she said, "but I like to be prepared, just in case."

"What are we making?" Charlotte asked, bouncing in her seat. "Tell me, tell me!"

"Well," said Claudia, "I thought we could see what it's like to make money."

"Counterfeiting?" asked Charlotte, looking very serious all of a sudden. "That's against the law."

"I know," said Claudia. "But we're not counterfeiting. We'll make the money much, much bigger than normal, so nobody could think we were actually trying to counterfeit. I just want to see how hard it really is."

116

"Do you think I should lock the door first?" asked Charlotte. "What if the police come?"

"If the police come, they'll be able to tell right away that we're just working on an art project," said Claud. "I promise you, it's safe. And fun!"

She pulled two dollar bills out of her pocket. "Here's your model," she said to Charlotte, giving her one. Then she tore off a sheet of drawing paper. "And here's our paper. We'll work on this together. Be sure to use the whole sheet of paper for our bill. That way it'll be too big to look real."

Charlotte started off slowly, but soon she was having a great time. Have you ever really looked at a dollar bill? It's a complicated object. Claudia told me it was one of the hardest things she had ever drawn.

Claud and Charlotte worked quietly, side by side. They drew George Washington in the middle of the paper. They drew the fancy 1's on each corner. They drew the special seal. Both of them were using fine-point black markers to sketch in the details; the color would come next.

Claud held her bill up to the light to see the red and blue fibers running through it. "I'll never be able to copy that," she said.

"What about these signatures?" asked Charlotte, pointing to the Treasurer's signature on one end and the Secretary of the Treasury's on the other. "I can't even read those names."

"Just scrawl something," said Claud. "It'll look close enough." She had moved on to the back of the bill, which was even more complicated. There was the pyramid with the eye on top of it and a lot more one's and 1's. Claud tried to count how many times the bill said "one" in different ways, but she kept losing track. There were a lot.

"What do these numbers on the front mean?" asked Charlotte, pointing to some lighter green numbers.

"Those are serial numbers," said Claud. "They can track the bills using those. They're for identification."

"This is fun," said Charlotte, "but it's hard. I think I'm going to make my own kind of money."

"Wow, great idea, Char," said Claudia. "This *is* hard. I wouldn't want to be a counterfeiter. You're right. It'll be a lot more fun to invent our own money."

They pushed their dollar bill aside and started over again with fresh paper. Charlotte made a "gazillion-dollar bill," with her picture in the middle. The bill was marked "Johanssenland," and it was signed by Charlotte as Queen. It was purple and blue, with touches of red.

Claudia made a wild, psychedelic bill using every color she could lay her hands on. "Land of Total Coolness," it said across the top. She included a picture of her favorite musical group in the middle, holding their guitars. "I wonder what would happen if we tried to spend these downtown," she said, giggling.

"They'd think we were crazy," replied Charlotte. "But wouldn't it be neat if money really could look like this? Real money is so boring."

"Other countries have neat money," said Claudia. "I saw this Canadian dollar bill once and it had a robin on it. It looked like play money."

"I bet our money looks like play money to people from other countries," said Charlotte thoughtfully.

"I bet you're right," agreed Claudia, impressed by Charlotte's reasoning. They finished their bills and put them aside.

"You guys haven't caught those counterfeiters yet, have you?" asked Charlotte. "Stacey could still be in trouble."

"We haven't caught them," Claudia admitted. "But I think Stacey will be okay."

"Couldn't we do some more spying?" asked Charlotte. "I really want to help."

Claudia checked her watch. "Your mom won't be back for over an hour," she said. "I guess we could go downtown." At our Monday meeting, we had decided that we should concentrate on watching the office supply store. It's different than the stationery store: it doesn't sell greeting cards or stickers or anything, just serious stuff like computer paper and manila envelopes and — copier supplies. We figured that anyone who was doing a lot of work on a copier would have to drop in for more supplies pretty often.

"Let's go!" said Charlotte. "Wait a minute, though. I have to get the official notebook." She ran to her room and brought back the notebook she and Jessi had bought. "Look, here are the notes we already have," she said, showing Claud. "I bet we get a lot more today."

They rode their bikes downtown and parked near the office supply store. "Okay," said Claudia, before they went in. "Remember, we're looking for men wearing hats indoors. And any other suspicious people."

"Right," said Charlotte, nodding.

They walked nonchalantly inside and started to act as if they were browsing. Charlotte looked at paper clips, and Claudia checked out the electric pencil sharpeners. Then Charlotte went to the pen-and-pencil section, and Claudia moved down the aisle to look over the weekly planner calendars. The stuff was pretty boring as far as Claud was concerned. No construction paper or poster paints. No glitter. No troll stickers. She had a hard time acting interested in file folders and blank computer disks.

"Can I help you?" asked a woman.

"Oh, uh," said Claudia. "I'm in this club, only it's more like a business. We're thinking of setting up an office to work out of." Claudia pictured the members of the BSC sitting in a real office, behind impressive desks, each with its own electric pencil sharpener, and she almost giggled.

"Well, just browse around, then," said the woman. "And if there's anything I can help you with, I'll be at the counter."

"Thanks," replied Claudia. She turned to a shelf full of pushpins and thumbtacks and tried to look fascinated. Then she heard the bell on the door to the store ring, and she turned to see who was coming in. It was a man — and he was wearing a hat! "Char!" Claudia hissed. Charlotte turned, and Claudia pointed as discreetly as she could. Almost immediately the man pulled off his hat and walked to the counter where calculators were displayed. He and the saleswoman began a conversation about the features of the various models. Claud looked at Charlotte and shrugged. Charlotte shrugged back.

Claudia returned to the pushpins. She had just decided that the brightly colored ones were kind of pretty when she heard a man behind her say, "Excuse me," as he reached for a pack of thumbtacks. The man had been in the store when Claudia and Charlotte came in, but Claudia had barely noticed him. He wasn't wearing a hat, for one thing. And he wasn't Mr. Fiske, whom Claudia was keeping an eye out for.

He was just a normal-looking guy, in jeans and a blue shirt. Not too tall, not too short, not too skinny or fat. Nobody you would notice, in other words.

Except.

Except for something that Claudia saw as he squeezed by her. "Cool," she said under her breath. She had seen a blue tattoo on his ear, at the spot where many people wear an earring. It was a small quarter moon next to a star. Claudia thought it was totally awesome. She almost tapped the man on the shoulder, so she could ask him about it, but then she realized that might be rude. Instead, she just stared at it, trying to figure out how it had been done. Did tattoos hurt? What if you wanted one that wasn't permanent?

Claudia pictured herself with a tattoo of a peace sign on her left earlobe. It would look outrageous, and she loved the idea. How could she do it? She thought hard. Blue food coloring would probably work, but how could she draw with that? Maybe she could use a toothpick that had been dipped in the dye. She wondered how long food coloring would take to wear off. Would she have to avoid showing her left side to her parents for a week? Two weeks? She knew they'd flip out if they saw a tattoo on her earlobe, even if it *wasn't* permanent. Claudia's parents are pretty cool about the clothes she wears, but she knew a tattoo would be pushing it.

Claudia was so deep in her thoughts that she barely noticed Charlotte pulling on her sleeve. The man had walked away by then, and was in a different part of the store. "Claudia!" Charlotte said.

"What, Char?" asked Claudia. "Did you see that cool tattoo?"

"Yup," said Charlotte. "I already wrote it down in the notebook."

Claudia nodded. "Good," she said, although it hadn't even occurred to her to make a note about the man. She was too fascinated by his tattoo.

"But that's not what I wanted to tell you," said Charlotte. "Look!" She pointed toward the counter. There was Mr. Fiske, talking to the saleswoman.

"Oh, my lord," said Claudia. She exchanged

looks with Charlotte, and the two of them started to edge closer to the counter, as unobtrusively as possible. Claudia didn't think Mr. Fiske would recognize her, since she's not in any of his classes, but she didn't want to take any chances. She strained her ears, trying to hear what he was saying.

" . . . need at least five cartridges of toner," he said.

"We may have to special order for that many," said the saleswoman. "But if you'll wait, I'll check our stockroom. You do know how much they cost, don't you?"

"I've budgeted plenty," he answered. "I know they cost a small fortune."

Charlotte and Claudia exchanged glances.

The woman left the counter and returned with a box in her hands. "I was able to find three," she said. "Check with me on Monday, and I should have the others by then."

Mr. Fiske paid — in cash! — and left. Claud and Charlotte left soon after. Charlotte stood on the sidewalk outside the store, scribbling furiously in the notebook. Mr. Fiske was up to something. Claud was sure of it. It wouldn't be long before the case of the mystery money was solved.

CHAPTER 12

"Did you bring the notebook?" asked Kristy.

"Got it," said Claudia. "I made sure to borrow it from Charlotte."

It was Friday afternoon. At Wednesday's BSC meeting, Claudia had told us what she and Charlotte had seen at the office supply store that day. Everybody had been very, very interested to hear about Mr. Fiske and the toner cartridges he was buying.

I'll admit that I might have been the most interested of all. After all, if we could prove that Mr. Fiske was the counterfeiter, Terry would be off the hook. I just *knew* Terry's family wasn't up to anything bad, but I couldn't prove that to anyone else. So I was hoping that Mr. Fiske was guilty. Isn't that terrible? I mean, he's a nice man and a pretty good teacher, even if he does wear silly ties sometimes. He also makes terrible jokes, which he seems to think spice up the class. Still, I didn't *really* want to see him get hauled off to prison. But if it was a choice between him and Terry, well, Terry was way too young — and too cute — to spend the rest of his life behind bars.

Anyway, we had decided on Wednesday that we would meet after school on Friday and spend some time tailing Mr. Fiske. ("Tailing" was Claudia's word. I think she got it from a Nancy Drew book.) Not everyone had been able to make it. Mallory and Mary Anne were sitting for Mal's younger brothers and sisters. Shannon was at the dentist again, and Dawn was attending the second session of her tofu cooking class. So it was just me, Claudia, Kristy, and Jessi. We met in the parking lot outside the gym as soon as the last classes of the day were over.

"Now, remember," said Kristy, "we don't want to be seen. Especially you, Stacey, since you're in his class."

"Yes, ma'am," I replied, saluting. Sometimes Kristy has to be reminded that she's being a little bit bossy. I grinned at her, and she grinned back.

"I'll be in charge of taking notes," said Claudia.

"Um," I said, "what if the rest of us want to be able to read them?"

Claudia giggled. She knows she's a terrible speller. "You're right," she said. She handed the notebook to Jessi, who has really nice handwriting. Also, she can spell.

"Where do you think he is right now?" asked Mary Anne.

"I saw him walking down the hall while I was at my locker," I said. "I think he was headed for the teachers' lounge."

"Good work," said Kristy. "That's where we'll go."

We trooped back into school and tiptoed down the hallway that leads to the auditorium. There's a mysterious room down that hall, with no window in the door, just a little sign on it that says, "Faculty Lounge." I've never quite figured out what teachers do in there. Do they really *lounge*? Like, do they lie around on couches and eat chocolates? Is it a pretty room, with decorative lamps and nice wallpaper and lots of big, comfortable chairs and the sweet smell of potpourri wafting through it? What happens if a student wanders into the room by accident? It's all a big mystery to me.

We stood outside the door of the lounge, trying to look as if we just happened to be hanging out there. For a long time, the door stayed shut. "I wonder if anybody is even in there," said Claudia. She walked up to the door and put her ear against it.

"Claudia!" I exclaimed, horrified. What if the vice-principal came out at that moment? She could get suspended or something.

"I heard voices," said Claudia, joining us again. "But I couldn't tell if Mr. Fiske was talking."

"What were they saying?" asked Kristy, looking very curious. I guess she's as mystified by the teachers' lounge as I am.

"I couldn't really hear," said Claudia. "Something about trading lunchroom duty next Wednesday."

Just then, the door swung open and a teacher I didn't recognize walked out. She glanced at us as she passed, but she didn't ask us anything.

"P.U.," said Jessi, holding her nose. We were standing close enough to the door so that we got a whiff of the smell inside the lounge, and it didn't smell like potpourri. "Cigarette smoke and stale coffee," said Jessi. "Delightful."

This gave me a new image of the lounge. There were probably six or seven plastic chairs and a ratty old brown couch. Fluorescent lights would beam down. A coffee machine would be sitting on an old student desk, with unwashed mugs next to it. I had a feeling that my new image was a lot closer to the truth than my old image had been.

"Psst!" Kristy hissed. "There he goes!" Mr. Fiske had just walked out of the lounge. Luckily, he was headed in the opposite direction, so he hadn't seen us. We took off after him, trying to act as if we were just strolling innocently down the hall.

Mr. Fiske walked along purposefully, past my locker, past Claudia's, past the drinking fountain. He slowed down a little and turned a corner, and then he disappeared into a classroom.

"That's his homeroom," I told the others. "Cokie Mason has him for homeroom, and she and her friends always watch to see what tie he's wearing that day. Then they make fun of it at lunchtime."

We clustered outside the door of the classroom. "Somebody peek inside to see what he's doing," said Claudia.

We all turned to look at her. She looked back at us, surprised. "Me?" she asked. "I have to do it?" She shrugged. "Okay." She inched over to the window that was set into the door, and then raised her head until she could just see inside. "He's rummaging around in his desk," she reported. "He looks like he's trying to find something important. He has this frown on his face."

"Maybe he keeps some of his fake money

in there," I whispered. "Is he pulling out any bills?"

Claudia shook her head. "Nope. Not yet, anyway." There was a pause while she watched him. "Oh!" she said, suddenly. "He pulled something out!"

"What is it?" we all asked at once. "What?"

"A red pencil," she breathed. "Maybe he uses it to put those little red lines onto bills."

I held my breath. Finally, we were on the brink of cracking the case.

"Oops," said Claudia, "never mind."

"What's he doing?" I asked.

"Correcting papers," she said. She turned to grin at me. "Did you take a quiz today?"

I nodded, remembering how hard it had been to concentrate on a multiple-choice test on *To Kill a Mockingbird* when my mind was full of counterfeiters.

"Maybe he's grading yours right now," whispered Claudia. "He's making lots of red marks."

"Oh, ha, ha," I said. "Very funny."

"Whoa!" said Claudia. "He's getting up. He's coming toward the door!" She ducked quickly, and we all scrambled away from the door. Mr. Fiske strode out and headed back down the hall, the way he had come.

"Maybe he's going to the basement!" Kristy

whispered. "You know, where the copier is?"

"Think he's going to run off a few thousand?" asked Jessi. "It would be so cool if we could catch him in the act."

But Mr. Fiske just kept walking, past the stairway that leads to the basement. He walked to a door, opened it, and went in. I was right behind him.

"Stacey!" Claudia hissed. "No!"

I turned to face her. "We're never going to catch him if we don't follow him," I said.

"But that's the men's room." Claud pointed to the sign. "I don't think you want to follow him *there!*"

I blushed. That was a close call. We waited outside the door until Mr. Fiske emerged. Then we followed him all the way *back* to his homeroom, and Claudia watched while he packed up his briefcase. "I guess he's going to mark the rest of those papers later," she said.

Mr. Fiske left his room and walked down the hall, back toward the stairway to the basement. I couldn't believe he hadn't spotted us yet, but he seemed preoccupied. I decided he was probably thinking about how much money he should make that night.

He paused at the head of the stairway,

looked at his watch, and then continued down the hall. "I guess he has enough money for today," Jessi whispered, giggling.

And that was it. We followed him out the main door, and watched him climb into his car. He owned a battered blue Honda. "It's not exactly a Cadillac, is it?" said Jessi as we watched him drive off.

"But just because we didn't catch him in the act doesn't mean he's innocent," I replied. I was still hoping.

"True," agreed Kristy. "But basically he seems like your average, everyday English teacher."

"Good cover," I said, under my breath.

"Well, we'll keep an eye on him," said Claudia. "Maybe he needs more supplies or something. Or maybe he's lying low. After all, he can't make money *every* day. He would look suspicious if he used the copier too much."

We split up, and I headed home to grab a snack before our BSC meeting. Just as I was taking the last bite of a banana, the phone rang. It was Terry.

"Hi!" I said, happy to hear from him.

"What have you been up to?" he asked.

And for some reason, the whole story about the counterfeiting and our detective work came spilling out. Well, not the whole story. I just told him that my friends and I were interested in the case, and that we wished we could solve it. I guess I wanted to feel him out, to see if he would take the bait. Maybe he'd end the suspense by breaking down and telling me that he and his family were the guilty ones. Of course, he didn't. But he did seem very, very interested in what I told him. He also seemed to know quite a bit about counterfeiting, which I thought was odd. He even knew about those tiny little red and blue lines.

Should I be happy that he knew so much? Maybe he could help us solve the case. Or should I be suspicious? After we had talked for a while and I hung up, I just stood there for a minute, thinking. I knew one thing for sure. I wasn't going to report this conversation at the meeting I was about to attend.

CHAPTER 13

"**W**ait, wait," said Charlotte. It was Saturday morning, and Charlotte and I were on our way downtown to do some sleuthing. Officially, I was baby-sitting for her, but unofficially we were McGill & Johanssen, Private Investigators. And one of the investigators had forgotten something. We had to double back to her house to get it.

"We can't do detective work without our notebook," said Charlotte, poking around her room to find it. "I can't believe I almost forgot it." She pulled it out from under her pillow, found a pen, and said she was ready to go.

We hit the sidewalk again and walked downtown without hurrying. It was a nice day. The sky was bright blue and there was just a little crispness in the air, enough to make you think of apples and sweaters and warm, cozy evenings by a fireplace. Charlotte skipped along beside me, singing "The Wheels on the Bus."

Downtown was busy that morning. People were dashing in and out of the stores, intent on their weekend errands. Charlotte and I stopped to look in a few windows, just for fun, on our way to the office supply store. "Sometimes I can almost understand why people make counterfeit money," Charlotte said with a sigh, gazing into the toy store window. She was looking at a gigantic teddy bear propped near a beautiful doll house. A china tea set with pink roses on it sat on a table nearby. "If I made my own money, I could buy everything I wanted," she said. "Wouldn't that be fun?"

"For awhile, maybe," I replied. "But you'd probably get bored pretty soon with having all that stuff." Then I thought of the red cowboy boots I had seen in a store window a few blocks back. They would look great with a full-length denim coat and a wide leather belt with silver medallions on it. I could think of a few things I wouldn't mind having, myself. And I'm not sure how soon *I* would get bored with buying everything I wanted. But I knew that counterfeiting wasn't the way to go.

When Charlotte and I arrived at the office supply store, we found that it was only open until noon. We wouldn't have much time to spy. Still, we hung around the copy machines, trying to appear as if we belonged there. I noticed that the woman behind the counter was beginning to look suspicious. I didn't blame her. I mean, it was a little odd that we had started to hang out there so much. She seemed busy with some paperwork, though, and she left us alone.

Unfortunately, it was a slow day at the office supply store. I guess they do most of their business during the week. A couple of people came in for little things like envelopes and paper, but that was it. Not one person looked at the new copiers, and nobody bought copy supplies.

At a quarter to twelve, I turned to Charlotte. "How about some lunch?" I asked. "We can grab a sandwich and then check out some other stores."

"Sure," she said. "Can we go to the Rosebud Cafe?"

I nodded, and we headed out the door and down the street. We decided to take a shortcut to the cafe, which meant crossing the parking lot in back of some stores. As we walked, we talked about what we planned to order for lunch. Suddenly, a young man ran across the parking lot — right toward us. He was running fast, and he kept looking over his shoulder. He hadn't seen us yet. I grabbed Charlotte and pulled her down behind the closest car. Somehow, I had a bad feeling about this man. He was running so wildly! Was he being chased?

Charlotte gasped when I grabbed her, but she squatted down quietly and we both watched the man as he dashed nearer to us. As he ran past us, we heard a thump, as though he had dropped something, something that sounded heavy. I ducked down to make sure he didn't see us. He paused for a half second, but then he ran on without picking up what he had dropped.

As soon as the man was out of sight, Charlotte started to stand up, but I pulled her back. "Somebody must be chasing him," I said. "Let's wait and see." But we waited for five minutes, and nobody showed up. Finally, when my heart had stopped beating like a drum, I stood up slowly and motioned to Charlotte to follow me.

We tiptoed out from behind the car and looked around to see what the man had dropped. "There!" cried Charlotte, pointing to a dirty white canvas bag. We walked toward it and examined it from a distance. It looked like a big laundry bag. I poked it gingerly, trying to figure out what might be in it. Not laundry, that was for sure. I felt hard edges, and corners.

"Let's open it," said Charlotte.

"Oh, I don't know," I said, nervously. But then my curiosity got the better of me. I picked up one corner of the bag and peeked inside. I nearly passed out when I saw what was in it.

"Money," breathed Charlotte. "Lots of it."

She was right. The bag was packed full of money. New bills, stacked tightly, with bands around them. I bent to look closer. The pack closest to me was one hundred-dollar bills! They were new and crisp and clean and — I touched one of them — totally smooth.

"It's money, all right," I said. "But it's not *real* money."

"You mean — ?" asked Charlotte.

"Right," I said. "It's counterfeit." My heart had started beating hard again.

"What should we do?" Charlotte asked.

"We *should* tell the police," I answered. "But we're not going to. I want to solve this case myself." I thought fast. "We'll stay here and stake out the area. There's no way he's going to leave all this money sitting in a parking lot. He'll be back. He may wait awhile, to make sure the coast is clear, but I'm sure he'll come back for this bag."

138

"I — I'm scared," said Charlotte.

"Me too," I admitted. "That's why I'm going to call Claudia and tell her to come down and wait with us. Maybe she can get some of our other friends, too. And I'll tell them to bring a camera. When that guy comes back, we'll be hiding nearby. We'll snap his picture, get it developed, and take it to the police. That'll be that!" I made it sound simple, but I knew it wasn't going to be easy. Still, I thought it was a good plan.

The first thing to do was call Claud. I looked around to make sure the man was nowhere in sight, and then Charlotte and I ran for the nearest pay phone, which was just across the parking lot. I called Claud and spit out the story as quickly as I could. I kept an eye on the money bag as I talked. "Hurry!" I said. "We'll be waiting for you." After I hung up, I thought for a minute. Then I took a deep breath and dialed Terry's number. I wasn't sure that calling him was the right thing to do, but I had a hunch that he could help us. I was sure, by now, that the Hoyts were not the counterfeiters. The man I'd seen was too young to be Mr. Hoyt. And Terry didn't even hesitate when I told him what was going on. He just said he was on his way.

Then Charlotte and I hid behind the red car again, the one I'd told Claud and Terry to look for. "I hope they get here soon," said Charlotte. "What if that guy comes back before we have the camera?"

"I don't know," I said. "I guess we'd have to follow him." That was not something I wanted to do. After all, he was a criminal. We wanted to stay as far away from him as possible. I crossed my fingers and waited for my friends, keeping a close eye on the parking lot. Charlotte looked excited and a little scared, which was exactly the way I felt. Were we finally about to catch the counterfeiters? I couldn't believe our big break had come while we were innocently crossing a parking lot, after all that time we'd spent staking out copy machines and following Mr. Fiske.

After a tense twenty minutes, Claudia showed up with Kristy and Jessi. Mary Anne was right behind them. I told them that Terry was coming, and made them promise not to act suspicious around him. After all, we seemed to have our suspect. They said they would be on their best behavior, and when Terry joined us a few minutes later they greeted him warmly.

"Did you bring the camera?" I asked Claudia. She nodded.

Kristy pulled me aside. "You know," she said, "I don't think Charlotte's parents would appreciate her being mixed up in this."

"I know," I said. "I've been thinking the same thing. But I don't know what to do about it."

"Jessi said she'd take Char back to her house to play with Becca," said Kristy. "We have enough people here to let her go, don't you think?"

"Definitely," I agreed. "Hey Char, can you come here?" Charlotte joined Kristy and me, and we told her we thought she should go home with Jessi. She looked disappointed for a second, and tried to talk us out of it, but then I thought she looked relieved.

"Okay," she said. "But will you call us right away if something happens?"

I promised I would.

After Jessi and Charlotte left, the rest of us huddled near the red car. The bag was still lying on the pavement in clear view. There was no way we could miss the man if he came back. I checked over the camera Claud had brought, making sure that there was film in it, that the battery had plenty of power, and that the automatic zoom lens was working.

"It's the end of a roll," Claudia said. "I was taking some pictures of flowers for a project I'm thinking about, but there are a few shots left."

"Great," I said. I held the camera ready, waiting for the man to come back. It was a long wait. People with shopping bags crossed the parking lot, heading for their cars. Other people drove in, parked, and headed for the stores. But the man didn't show up. Luckily, nobody came for the red car we were still hiding behind. We waited patiently, and then not so patiently.

"When's he going to come?" asked Claudia. "I should have brought a sketchpad with me so I wouldn't be wasting all this time."

"Here, you can draw on this," I said, handing her Charlotte's spy notebook. "Charlotte left it behind."

"The paper's too small," said Claud. "And I don't have my good pens with me. Plus, there's nothing much to sketch, really. But thanks, anyway." She handed the notebook back, and I started to flip through it, just to pass the time.

Most of the handwriting in the book was terrible, since the notes had been jotted down while the writer was standing around spying. I strained to read a note near the beginning. "Hey, this is funny," I said to Claud. "Didn't you say you saw a man with a blue tattoo one day? Here's another note about him. Somebody else saw him, too." I showed her the page. "I can't tell whose handwriting it is."

Claudia peered at the page. "It might be Becca's," she said. "Huh, that's — "

"Shhhh!" said Terry suddenly. Claud and I turned to look at him. He was pointing at something. I poked my head up over the back bumper of the car to see what it was. It was the man! He was back for his bag of cash, and he was only a few yards away from where we were hiding. I grabbed behind me for the camera, and Claudia put it in my hand. I raised it over the bumper, pointed it at the man, checked through the viewfinder to make sure I had him in the frame, and snapped three pictures as quickly as I could while he bent to pick up the bag. My hands were shaking so hard that I could hardly hold the camera still.

The man looked around after he'd picked up the bag. We ducked down quickly, and he didn't spot us. Then he hurried off.

"Did you get the pictures?" Kristy asked.

I nodded. "I think so," I said.

"All *right!*" said Terry, giving me the high-five. We were all grinning like maniacs.

"Now what happens?" asked Mary Anne.

"I'll take the film to be developed at that quickie place," I said. "As soon as we get the pictures back we can take them to the police. It might take a couple of hours, though."

"A couple of *hours?*" asked Claudia.

"You guys don't have to stay," I said. "I can take care of it. Go on home, and I'll call you as soon as the pictures are ready."

So my friends left, but Terry decided to keep me company.

"It's nice of you to stay," I said to Terry as we walked toward the photo store. I felt a little shy with him all of a sudden.

"That's okay," he replied. He started to say something else, but then he stopped.

"What is it?" I asked.

"Stacey," he said, looking very serious, "when we get those pictures developed, we don't have to go to the police."

"What do you mean?" I asked. "How else can we — "

"We can just take them to my father," he interrupted. "He'll take care of everything."

I froze. "Take care of everything"? What did Terry mean? Maybe his family *was* involved in making the mystery money. And now, maybe they were about to get rid of me — *permanently* — because I knew too much.

CHAPTER 14

"Your *father*?" I repeated. "What are you talking about?"

"He — I mean, I — oh, man," said Terry. "It's a long story. Let's drop off the film first, and then I'll tell you all about it."

I was incredibly curious, and also pretty scared, but I could see that Terry wasn't ready to explain himself yet. I led the way to the camera store and gave the film to the woman behind the counter. She said the pictures would be ready in a little over an hour. We left the store, and as we walked down the street I turned to Terry. "So what's going on?" I asked.

"You know what?" he said. "I'm totally starved. How about if we get something to eat?"

We had to wait for the pictures anyway, so I figured we might as well. Besides, I had suddenly realized that I was incredibly hungry myself, even if I *was* about to be rubbed out. We headed for the pizza place and ordered some vegetarian slices and two sodas. (Diet for me, of course.) I started to look around for a table, but Terry steered me toward the door.

"Let's eat out in the park," he said. "I can't talk in here."

We found a bench in a sunny spot and sat down to eat. For a few minutes, we just concentrated on our pizza. Then, when my stomach had stopped growling and my curiosity had gotten the better of me, I looked at Terry and said, "Okay, what did you want to tell me?"

He stared down at his pizza. "It's like this," he said. He stopped and heaved a big sigh. "Oh, man, I can't believe I'm telling you this." He paused again.

"Telling me *what*? You haven't said anything yet."

"I know," he said. "Stacey, this is really hard for me. You'll have to be patient."

I sat back and folded my arms. "Okay," I said. "Whenever you're ready."

"It's just kind of hard to explain." Terry looked down at his pizza again. He seemed to be fascinated with it, but I knew he was just stalling. "See, the thing is, my father has kind of a strange job," he said finally. "He's with the Secret Service."

I gasped. "You're kidding!" I cried.

"Nope," Terry said, shaking his head. "I know it sounds like something out of a James Bond movie, but it's true. My father is an undercover government agent." He was talking in a really low voice, so I had to strain to hear him. He was also looking around, as if checking to make sure nobody could overhear him. "His job is to infiltrate areas where counterfeiters are operating. He works on each case until it's solved, which can take anywhere from a few weeks to a few years. Then he moves on. We all move on."

My head was spinning. "You mean — you mean that's why you moved here?" I asked. I was feeling incredibly relieved. I wasn't going to be rubbed out after all.

He nodded.

"And — and that's why you knew so much about counterfeiting?" I asked.

He nodded again. "I was kind of worried when I heard you and your friends were involved. Counterfeiters can be tough criminals," he said. "They don't like anyone getting in their way. But I couldn't tell you about my father, since his identity has to be a secret. Now you really may be on to something, though, and I think you should talk directly to him instead of going to the police first."

I was still thinking, hard. "So, this is why

your family hasn't unpacked yet?" I asked. "Because you may be moving on soon?" I felt a pang at the thought of Terry leaving, just when I was getting to know him better.

"That's right," he said. "I don't think I've ever lived in one place for more than a couple of years."

"And do you change your name when you move?" I asked, thinking of his two middle names — and of Tasha's ID with another name on it.

"Uh-huh," he said. "Sometimes it's hard to remember who I'm supposed to be. We have drills when we get our new names. Dad fires questions at us, like, 'What's your name? What's your brother's name?' and we have to answer really quickly. We just say the names over and over again until we feel comfortable with them." He looked kind of lost and sad.

"Will you tell me your real name?" I asked. "The one you were born with?"

"Why?"

"I just want to know it. So I know the real you."

Terry took my hand. "Stacey — " he said, and then he stopped and looked deep into my eyes. "My name is David Hawthorne," he said finally. "Dave."

"David," I repeated softly. "Hi, David."

He gave me a sad smile. "Hi, Stacey," he said. "I'm glad to meet you."

We laughed, but Terry — David? — still looked sad. I guess his life isn't an easy one, with all that moving around. I could hardly imagine it, even though I've moved a few times myself. What about friendships? What about — relationships?

"Hey, it's time to pick up those pictures," said Terry. (I'll just call him that to make it simpler.) He stood up and stretched, looking relieved at having finally spilled his big secret.

"Great!" I said. "Let's go."

He grabbed my arm. "Stacey," he said. "Thanks."

"For what?"

"For being understanding. And for asking me my real name."

I smiled at him. "Thank *you*," I said. "For telling me the truth." We headed for the camera store, holding hands.

Terry and I picked up the pictures, and I took them out of the envelope before we had even left the store. I couldn't wait to see what our counterfeiter looked like. I knew he had brown hair and that he was about average height, but that was all I'd seen. I had been too busy snapping pictures to notice much else.

I pulled Terry over to a bench outside the store and we sat down to flip through the pictures. "He doesn't *look* like a criminal," I said when I'd found the first one I'd taken.

"Most counterfeiters don't," said Terry. "They tend to look pretty normal."

"This guy could be my next-door neighbor," I said, flipping to the next picture. Then I saw something that made me gasp. "Except," I said, "that my next-door neighbor doesn't have a blue tattoo of a moon and a star on his ear!"

"Let me see," said Terry, taking the picture. "Wow!" he said. "That should make identification pretty easy."

"I can't believe it," I said. "This has got to be the same guy Claudia saw. That's wild."

"I never understand why people get tattoos if they're going to be criminals," said Terry. "Like, you know those posters in the post office? The ones that say 'Wanted'? I mean, half of those guys have tattoos all over their bodies. Doesn't seem smart, does it?"

"Nope," I said, grinning. "But I'm not complaining. Mr. Blue Tattoo must be our man, and now we have proof! Let's go show these to your dad."

Terry found a pay phone and called his father to ask him to pick us up. "He says he'll meet us on the corner near Bellair's," he said.

We walked over there and waited until a white car pulled up. "Hi, Dad," said Terry as we climbed in.

"Hi, Terry," said the man driving the car. Then he turned to me. "Hello, Stacey," he said.

My mouth dropped open. The man in the front seat was one of the "officers" who had questioned me at the police station that afternoon. He had been the one who seemed to be in charge, the one who was dressed in a regular suit instead of a uniform. "Uh — hi!" I said. As soon as I recovered from the shock, I realized it made perfect sense that Mr. Hoyt would have been involved in the questioning.

"Let's head on home before we talk," said Mr. Hoyt. "Terry tells me you may have some interesting information."

I nodded. "I do, I think," I said. I sat back in my seat and tried to calm down as we drove to the Hoyts'. I suddenly realized that trusting Terry could have been dangerous. I had believed him right away when he told me his father was an undercover agent, and it had turned out that he had been telling the truth. But what if Mr. Hoyt actually had been the counterfeiter? I could have been walking straight into a trap. Was it luck? Or was I a good judge of character? Anyway, I knew now that Terry's father *was* who Terry had said he was, and that from here on he could take over. My friends and I had done a lot of work — good work — on the case, and now it was time to let the professionals step in. Finally, I could relax.

When we reached the Hoyts', Terry's dad led me into a little den that was off the living room. Terry joined us and sat on a leather chair, and his dad sat on another. Mr. Hoyt asked me to sit on the couch. "Okay, Stacey," he said. "I understand that you have some pictures for me to see. But first, I'd like you to tell me what you and your friends have been doing since the last time I saw you. Terry tells me that you've been up to some detective work."

"That's true," I said. "I wanted to clear my name after I got hauled in to the police station."

"In my book, your name was always clear," he replied. "But I understand. Go on."

I told him about our work on the case. I explained about Charlotte and her spy notebook, and about staking out copiers and the office supply store. Then I remembered about tailing Mr. Fiske. "Oh, no!" I said, putting my hand over my mouth. "I can't believe we thought it was my English teacher." I told Mr. Hoyt about following Mr. Fiske all over school.

"As long as he didn't see you, he'll never

know you suspected him," said Mr. Hoyt, grinning.

"I hope you're right. I would be so embarrassed if he knew."

"Now," said Mr. Hoyt. "Tell me what happened today."

I told him how Charlotte and I had gone downtown, and what we had done there. Then I told him about the running man and the bag full of money. "So I called my friends, and they brought a camera downtown, and we waited for the guy to come back, and we got his picture!" I held up the envelope. I felt pretty proud of myself.

Mr. Hoyt looked stern. "You know, don't you, that you put yourself in great danger by acting as you did?" he said. "Catching counterfeiters is not a game. You should have informed the police as soon as you found that bag of money." He turned to Terry. "And you should never have let them wait for that man to come back," he said. "You know better, son."

Terry and I tried to look serious. "We know it was wrong," I said. "But wait till you see these pictures."

"I'm sorry, Dad," Terry added. "I just felt I couldn't interfere then." Mr. Hoyt nodded at Terry, and then he turned to me.

"All right, then," he said. "Let's see what

you've got." I handed him the pictures, and he looked at each in turn. "Hmmm," he said. "Interesting."

I pointed to one of the pictures. "What about this?" I asked. I was pointing to the blue tattoo.

"Ah," said Mr. Hoyt. "The blue tattoo. Just what we needed."

"Needed?" I asked. "For what?"

"It may be the piece of evidence that we were missing," said Mr. Hoyt. "We've been narrowing down the scope of our investigation, focusing on several known counterfeiters. This man is one of them, and this may be enough to bring him in." Mr. Hoyt stood up. "Stacey, I want to thank you for your help. Your procedures were incorrect and dangerous, but they may have been successful. Now that we know exactly who we're after, my guess is that we'll have our man within a few days." He shook my hand and hurried off.

"Wow!" I said, turning to Terry.

"I think you've caught a counterfeiter," said Terry, giving me a high-five.

We smiled at each other. Then I checked my watch. "I should get home, I guess," I said.

"Wait," said Terry. "I have to talk to you about something."

"Another secret?" I asked, raising my eyebrows. "I thought I knew them all."

154

Terry looked serious. "Not another secret. Just more about the one I already told you. The thing is, I didn't tell my dad that I told you who he is. I pretended I just told you he was a police officer. If he knew I had told you everything . . ." Terry looked pale. "You have to promise me you'll never tell anyone what I told you. You could put our lives in jeopardy if you did."

I nodded. "I understand," I said.

"I don't know if you really *can* understand, but thanks. I never should have told you my family's secret, because now it's yours, too. I'm sorry. My whole life is one big secret, and I guess it was suddenly just too much for me. I couldn't help telling you."

I crossed the room and put my hand on his shoulder. "You have my promise, David," I said. "I'll never tell a soul." He smiled up at me. It wasn't going to be easy, but I knew I would keep my pledge.

CHAPTER 15

I hate lying to people. It's something I never do. Well, almost never. But this was a special case. I had made a promise to Terry, and I had to keep it. So I didn't even tell Claudia, my best friend in the world, the whole truth. When I called her that night, I tried not to tell her any actual lies. Instead, I did what my mother calls "lying by omission." That means that instead of telling an untruth, you just leave things out. For instance, I told Claudia that Mr. Hoyt was in charge of the counter-feiting case, and that he was "some sort of police officer." I *didn't* tell her what he really did for a living. I just left that part out.

Claudia, along with my other friends, seemed a little miffed at me for going directly to Mr. Hoyt. "I mean," said Claudia, "even if he *is* in charge and everything, you could have called us. We wanted to be there when you showed those pictures to the authorities."

"I know," I said. "I just thought it was better to act quickly."

"But we were all working on the case," said Claud. "I mean, who brought you the camera? If you hadn't had that, you wouldn't have been able to take any pictures."

"I know, I know. And I'm really grateful to you for everything you did. But isn't the most important thing that the case might be solved soon?"

"I guess you're right. I still would have liked to be there." Claud sounded hurt, and I could understand why she felt left out. But there wasn't anything I could do about it.

I spent a tense four days after that, waiting for news about the case. Claudia — and everyone else — had forgiven me, but they still weren't acting as friendly as usual. Then, after supper on Tuesday evening, I got a phone call.

"Stacey? This is Mr. Hoyt." I was so surprised that I didn't know what to say. "I just wanted to let you know that, with your help, the counterfeiters have been captured. It will be in the news tomorrow."

"Wow!" I exclaimed.

"The man you took pictures of was wanted for several other crimes. He and a couple of his pals are already safely behind bars."

"That's great!"

"The work that you and your friends did

was very helpful," said Mr. Hoyt, "and I want to thank you. But I also want to warn you against getting involved in a case like this again. What you did could have been very dangerous."

"I know. I'm sorry. I guess we got carried away."

"Well, it ended okay," he said. "Now, I think there's someone here who would like to talk to you, so I'll say good-bye."

Terry got on the phone. "Hi, Stacey," he said. "I was wondering if you could meet me somewhere for a few minutes. I want to talk to you."

We agreed to meet at the playground at the elementary school, and fifteen minutes later I was sitting on a swing, Terry beside me on the next swing. It was pretty dark out by then, and it felt strange to be at the playground at night. Strange, but kind of special, too.

"So, congratulations," said Terry.

"Thanks," I replied. "Is that all you wanted to tell me?"

"No," he admitted. "I wanted to see you so I could say good-bye."

"You've leaving?" I felt shocked, even though I had known this would happen.

He nodded. "Very soon, probably," he said. "We never stick around after a case is solved. We're packed already, and we'll be on our way as soon as Dad has his next assignment." He reached over and took my hand. "I wish we didn't have to go," he said.

"So do I," I answered, squeezing his hand. "But I'll always remember you — David."

He smiled that sad smile again. Then he jumped up from the swing, and pulled me up off mine. Then he gave me a kiss — maybe the sweetest kiss I've ever had. "I'll always remember you, too," he said. "I've never met anyone like you, Stacey."

I looked into those hazel eyes for a long moment. "Will you write to me?" I asked.

He shook his head. "I can't. Too dangerous. But somehow I think we may meet again."

"I hope so." We kissed again. "And don't worry about your secret," I said. "It's safe with me." Terry gave me a big hug, and then we said good-bye. I walked home, feeling a strange, bittersweet sadness. I probably wouldn't have the chance to get to know Terry better. But I was really glad I had met him, and I knew I'd never forget him.

The next morning, the story of the counterfeiters — and their capture — was all over the news. COUNTERFEITERS NABBED shouted the headline in the paper. The morning news on TV covered the story, too.

I read the newspaper article carefully. It didn't mention me or my friends, but I hadn't expected it to. After all, the operation had been pretty much top secret. It didn't mention Mr. Hoyt, either, at least not by name. The article talked about an undercover government agent, who, acting on "tips given by alert civilians," had cracked the case of the mystery money.

Alert civilians. That was me and my friends. Pretty cool. The man with the blue tattoo had been caught, along with several of his buddies, when they walked into a trap set up by Mr. Hoyt and the police. It was a sting operation. The criminals were set up to believe that they were going to be able to convert a lot of their counterfeit bills into real cash. Apparently, Mr. Hoyt had posed as an "underworld figure" who was willing to take the fake bills off their hands.

It worked like a charm.

At school that day, everybody was talking about the case. And when I got home that afternoon, Charlotte called to tell me how glad she was to find out that my name had finally been cleared.

That afternoon at our BSC meeting, we talked about how amazing it had been that the criminals had been nabbed. "I didn't think much of Charlotte's little notebook," Kristy admitted. "It was, like, just a fun game. But all that work paid off."

"Stacey's the one who really cracked the case," said Claudia. She pulled something out from under her bed. "Here, Stace, I made this for you. So you'll never forget your first counterfeiting case."

First and last, I thought to myself. And I knew I'd never forget it anyway. I took the package Claudia handed me and unwrapped it. Inside was a framed painting of a "counterfeit" bill. It was a large red, white, and blue bill, with a great sketch of me in the middle. "This is terrific!" I said. Now I knew that Claudia had completely forgiven me.

"Just don't spend it all in one place," Claud said, grinning.

We cracked up.

"I'll hang it over my bed," I said. "I love it. Thanks, Claud."

Then the phone started ringing, and we spent the next few minutes lining up jobs.

"I wonder why Mrs. Hoyt hasn't called," said Kristy, after awhile. "She told me last week that she thought she was going to need a regular sitter for Georgie."

"Didn't you hear?" said Mary Anne. "The Hoyts moved away. To Arizona, I think. Or maybe it was New Mexico. Tasha wasn't in gym class today, and somebody told me that she and her family were already gone. I think they left today."

Everybody turned to look at me, since they knew how I felt about Terry.

Did you know they were leaving?" Kristy asked.

I shrugged. "Terry said they might," I answered.

"Why did they go?" asked Dawn.

"I don't know," I said, thinking that I wasn't exactly lying. I didn't know what Mr. Hoyt's next assignment was, after all. "Maybe Mrs. Hoyt was offered a job there or something." For all I knew, that might be true.

"What about you and Terry?" asked Claudia.

I shrugged again. "I guess it just wasn't meant to be. It was one of those short but sweet romances."

I heard Mal and Jessi sigh. They must have thought that sounded romantic. Well, I guess it was. Terry had swept into my life and then left suddenly. It was like something out of a book.

When our meeting broke up, I took my painting and headed home to hang it on the wall. I called Claudia to tell her how great it looked. I also told her a little about my good-bye scene with Terry (not the secret stuff, of course), and how he had kissed me.

"He sure was cute," said Claudia.

"He was really nice, too," I said. "I mean,

his looks may have attracted me to him in the first place, but it was his personality that made him great."

"Not to mention his kissing technique," said Claud. I could tell, even over the phone, that she was grinning.

We hung up soon afterward, and I tried to do some homework. But it was hard to concentrate. I kept thinking about Terry, and how hard his life must be. But his life was exciting, too, and he got to meet interesting people everywhere he went. I knew he'd be okay, and I also knew he was probably right about our meeting again. I had the same feeling.

I was so deeply involved with my day-dreaming that I almost jumped out of my seat when the phone rang. I ran into Mom's room to answer it. It was Sam Thomas, of all people.

"Sam!" I said. "How are you?"

"I'm okay. I heard about your work on that counterfeiting case. Pretty awesome."

"Thanks." I hesitated. Sam sounded as if he wanted to talk about something else. "What's new with you?" I asked.

"Nothing. I mean, well — " He hesitated. "Stace, I really miss you," he blurted out.

"You *do*? What about what's-her-name? I mean, Kathy?"

"She's okay," said Sam. "But we're not serious or anything. I don't know, Stacey. I like dating other people, but I still like you a lot, too."

"Oh, Sam," I said. "I like you, too. I know exactly what you mean."

"So what do we do?" he asked.

"I don't know. I guess we just keep going on this way. I mean, we can still date each other once in awhile, but we can feel free to see other people, too." I didn't know if there was anybody I wanted to "see," now that Terry was gone, but I knew I wanted to feel that I could if I wanted to.

"Cool," said Sam. "How about going out this Friday?"

"Sounds great," I said. And that was that.

After I'd hung up, I lay on my bed for awhile and tried to figure everything out. It had been a crazy couple of weeks. I had (unknowingly) passed a counterfeit bill. I had helped to solve a mystery. I had worked things out (maybe!) with Sam. I had met a wonderful new boy, and then I had said good-bye to him. And, last but definitely not least, I had learned a secret that I would have to keep forever. It was David Hawthorne's secret — and now it was my secret, too.

About the Author

ANN M. MARTIN did *a lot* of baby-sitting when she was growing up in Princeton, New Jersey. She is a former editor of books for children, and was graduated from Smith College.

Ms. Martin lives in New York City with her cats, Mouse and Rosie. She likes ice cream and *I Love Lucy*; and she hates to cook.

Ann Martin's Apple Paperbacks include *Yours Truly, Shirley*; *Ten Kids, No Pets*; *With You and Without You*; *Bummer Summer*; and all the other books in the Baby-sitters Club series.

Look for Mystery #11

CLAUDIA AND THE
MYSTERY AT THE MUSEUM

"Please explain yourself," the museum curator said sternly, ignoring my red cheeks.

"Well, it — it's just that I noticed something strange about one of the Don Newman pieces," I said. I told him all about how I had seen — and touched — the sculpture before, and about how it seemed different now. "Maybe somebody switched it during the robbery or something. I just think it may be a fake; I mean, a forgery," I finished, looking at the floor. Somehow I knew he wasn't going to believe me.

I was right. "This is the most absurd thing I've ever heard," Mr. Snipes said, rolling his eyes. He pushed a button on his intercom. "Ms. Hobbes, bring me the Newman file," he said into it. Then he looked back at me and Stacey. "Playing detective may be an amusing way to pass an afternoon," he said, "but taking up *my* time with your ridiculous theories is pushing things a little too far." Ms. Hobbes brought in the file, and he showed me the registration number for the sculpture. Then he marched us down to the gallery and showed us that the number matched the one on the artwork. Afterwards, we went back to his office. "I hope you've enjoyed your little game," he said. "And I trust I won't be seeing you in here again."

"No, sir. We're very sorry, sir," said Stacey.

I didn't say anything. I was too busy sneaking a piece of paper off his desk while Stacey apologized. It was a copy of Mr. Snipes's résumé. There were several lying there, and somehow I was suddenly overcome by the need to know more about this nasty man. I know it wasn't the *right* thing to do, but right or not, I had to do it. There was something rotten going on in that museum, and I wanted to get to the bottom of it.

**Don't miss any of the latest books
in the Baby-sitters Club series
by Ann M. Martin**

#60 *Mary Anne's Makeover*
Everyone loves the new Mary Anne — *except* the BSC!

#61 *Jessi and the Awful Secret*
Only Jessi knows what's really wrong with one of the girls in her dance class.

#62 *Kristy and the Worst Kid Ever*
Need a baby-sitter for Lou? Don't call the Baby-sitters Club!

#63 *Claudia's Friend Friend*
Claudia and Shea can't spell — but they can be friends!

#64 *Dawn's Family Feud*
Family squabbles are one thing. But the Schafers and the Spiers are practically waging war!

#65 *Stacey's Big Crush*
Stacey's in LUV . . . with her twenty-two-year-old teacher!

#66 *Maid Mary Anne*
Mary Anne's a baby-sitter — not a housekeeper!

#67 *Dawn's Big Move*
Dawn's moving back to California. But she'll be back, right?

Super Specials:

8 *Baby-sitters at Shadow Lake*
Camp fires, cute guys, *and* a mystery — the Baby-sitters are in for a week of summer fun!

SPECIAL DELIVERY... FOR YOU!

The Baby-sitters have split up for vacation, but Kristy's in the hospital. How will the girls stay in touch?—A chain letter! Now *you* can open authentically stamped envelopes, unfold and read real letters in the baby-sitters' own hand—writing, and learn a special secret about each one of them — all in one spectacular, must—have book!

Real letters, cards, and even a friendship bracelet from the Baby-sitters Club!

The Baby-Sitters Club Chain Letter
by Ann M. Martin

Coming in September!

Create Your Own
Mystery Stories!

MYSTERY GAME !

WHO: Boyfriend   **WHY:** Romance

WHAT: Phone Call   **WHERE:** Dance

Use the special Mystery Case card to pick WHO did it, WHAT was involved, WHY it happened and WHERE it happened. Then dial secret words on your Mystery Wheels to add to the story! Travel around the special Stoneybrook map gameboard to uncover your friends' secret word clues! Finish four baby-sitting jobs and find out all the words to win. Then have everyone join in to tell the story!